GRANDDADDY WAS ALWAYS A *kid* AT HEART

GRANDDADDY WAS ALWAYS A *kid* AT HEART

LEONARD N. BEARDSLEY

TATE PUBLISHING & *Enterprises*

Published by Tate Publishing & Enterprises, LLC
127 E. Trade Center Terrace | Mustang, Oklahoma 73064 USA
1.888.361.9473 | www.tatepublishing.com

Tate Publishing is committed to excellence in the publishing industry. The company reflects the philosophy established by the founders, based on Psalm 68:11,
"The Lord gave the word and great was the company of those who published it."

Book design copyright © 2011 by Tate Publishing, LLC. All rights reserved.
Cover design by Leah LeFlore
Interior design by Joey Garrett

Published in the United States of America

ISBN: 978-1-60462-633-9
1. Fiction
2. Christian
11.10.12

This book is dedicated to all seniors and their caregivers everywhere, to my mother, grandmother, brother, and cousin for their encouragement and insight for improvements. I thank God for the talent and words that went to print. Also, thanks to Tate Publishing for their patience.

CHAPTER 1

Granddaddy was always a kid at heart. Even with his car, an old Packard, he acted like a kid. The Packard was his most prized possession except for Coon, his old hound dog. Yes, Granddaddy was just one of the gang until he got really old. He caught more kites in a tree than even the littlest tykes in town and competed to see who would crash one first, instead of how high it would go. Granddaddy was eighty.

One day there was a thunderstorm, and everyone ran to hide in the barn except you-know-who. Guess he thought he'd be Ben Franklin, Junior, but he wasn't. When a lightning bolt like was never seen jolted out of the black-as-a-cave cloud to hit him slam on top of his bald head, havoc reigned, and little spikes of electricity crept along the ground all around him for what looked like an acre. From the shock of it all, corn wilted. Well, the only harm to Granddaddy that seemed to come of it all was his straw hat.

Or what was left of it. From the cracked-open door, all watched as one thread of straw fluttered to the ground, spinning like one of those maple seeds does. Wagging his head as Coon did when trying to jerk a stick from you, he shouted, "Whoo we, that was one bull of a wagon ride!"

Willie was his twelve-year-old grandson and the star in Gramp's eyes. To Willie, there was only one of a kind like Granddaddy. So he said, "Grandma can wait for you in the hereafter. We've told her that we need you now, so guess she must have said, 'oh well' to that one, Gramps. Granddaddy, what made you think you're a lightning rod? That metal plate in your noggin that you got when they fixed you after that car crash?" asked Will.

"W," as he sometimes called Will, "I haven't been around eighty years 'cause I let young ones tell me how to keep alive. We're not going until we're called." And that was how he felt about his age. Getting the wind from his bag sometimes, the preacher simply nodded his head in respect. After all, Cyrus McGinn was the last real Scotsman in town, and most remembered the whipping they or someone they knew received from the grizzled old carpenter years ago.

Cracking fun, Will said, "Grandpa, glad my hair turned green when I dyed it to get the red out a few years ago. Now, a lot of the students call me tree and rename me by the kind they feel that I am on a day. It's been a better life since then."

Sally Lu was one of the two of Will's friends who hid in the barn from the storm and the wisest eleven-year-old kid in Greentown, a mecca of peace and congeniality in Georgia. Her eyes were sky-blue, and people thought they often saw the clouds reflected in them. Like a beacon in the darkness, her snow-white blonde hair often startled people who thought she was a ghost.

CHAPTER 2

"Will," she said, "you know not to let the crude people disturb you. When their actions bother you, they may agitate you more. We can all be taunted by others. Your hair color is rare, that's all. Like yourself and earn their respect in other ways, such as assisting those, whether kids or adults, with tasks they can't do alone."

Shannon, a freckled guy of age twelve, was the older of Will's two friends. Always meditative but with a jolly side, he grinned through hardships. At nearly six feet tall, he dreamed to be a pro basketball player but to help the poor with his money. When he wasn't dunking a basketball through a hoop, he'd reading. It was usually some paperback stuffed in his back pocket. But he loved his family and friends. Since he didn't have a grandfather, Cyrus was like his own. It was like he had two families, one he played with and one he stayed with.

"Grandpa Cy," as he called him, "you're the youngest

of us, you know, as we never see you tucker out and ole' Will probably couldn't even outrun you. Nobody's like you, for sure, and we've got to keep you around until the earth stops."

"Shannon," Cy said while he scratched his head with about two hairs on it, "sometimes I want to adopt you, steal you right out from under your dad and mom and finish raising one more to give me a real reason to be here to one hundred. Even with Coon's companionship and Will's visits every few days, that house with an empty room is too bare. Houses are for filling, with kids, wives, animals and love. Yep, that's what's wrong. I've still got some extra heart that needs to be spent on somebody."

"What about the church, Grandpa?" asked Sally Lu. "Can't they put that heart to use helping the Lord in some way? Maybe there are ill folks you could visit, or aren't there some older ladies who might be alone you could be friends with, maybe even marry someday?"

"Well Sal," he said, "at the church I'm spending hours already, working harder than the preacher sometimes. If I get done too fast, he's likely out of work, too. Seems about time I visit the sick, they perk up, like I'm embarrassing them for being down when I wait on them. And I've liked a few ladies, lately Hilda, who shied away after months because of the memories of their husbands who passed away, usually. The younger ones—well, that bouncing and giggling like high school girls often puts my mind on the blink. Guess I could learn to love them, but I might need pep pills to handle the perkies all the time."

"Oh Gramps," said Shannon, "I wish we had room to just tuck you and Coon into the house, and you know that after Will's dad, Dad's the best carpenter in Greentown. An extra part of the house built on would be a snap, and you could go to your place anytime 'cause you know that we could use a new grandpa. Mom and Dad still talk about Grandpa Sam, though he's been gone two years when he followed Ma Mary because he missed her so. How about comin' with us right away?"

"Hey, are you trying to take my grandpa?" Will snapped, lunging at Shannon, skirting the big boy and tumbling right into a brier bush. "Owww! Get these thorns out of my hide. I'm not a cow, you know." Hunching over him, Shannon and Sally gingerly pulled the sticky branches from his shorts and skin. A few were close to his eyes, and Will shivered as each piece was pulled away and then snipped with Gramp's pocketknife.

After taking karate for three years, Will was a tough character. He arose from the brier patch and sprung at Shannon with a side kick that struck him in the stomach. Then Shannon said, "Will McGinn, I'm going to whip the rest of that Scottish blood out of you that the briers didn't get." His face reddened with rage and he wept. Sidestepping Shannon's haymaker punch, Will swept his open hand against his ribs. Shannon bowled over in pain.

Sally Lu said, "Stop it, Will. You'll kill him!"

Ignoring her, Will lunged for Shannon's legs. When Will missed and Shannon slapped him to the ground, Will said, "Shannon, we've been friends a long time, but we can become enemies."

"You're Scottish, and I'm Irish. Expect it," Shannon grunted. "I loved to fight before I moved here. The place is too tidy, and it needs some dirt," he said with a smirk.

Responding with a front snap kick to Shannon's chest and then a back-fist to his head, Will slammed Shannon to the ground like Goliath. "Sorry Shannon, but when one wins, the other loses." Walking over to Sally Lu, Will mumbled, "Girls don't like violence, and I don't either. But our sensei or karate master told us to 'try to walk away if you can, but if you can't, use all of your skills to defend yourself. Have pride, win or lose, and carry your head high.' That's what I did, and I trust you'll forgive me." He grinned.

"I can forgive, but forgetting is another thing. You didn't try hard enough to walk away. But I'll walk away from you now. When your heart heals, give me a call," Sally chided. Glaring at them, Sally, always the peacemaker, admitted, "This is only the fourth time in years that Shannon and Will have fought, and boys can be aggressive. Will monopolizes Cy. And Shannon feels as if Cy's his second dad. Not many of us are lucky enough to have two, but I'm surprised he doesn't live at Will's house." Pirouetting and plodding to Slow Creek, where she could meditate, tears streamed down her face as she mourned the loss of a friend. On the way, she eyed Cy and sighed, "Why aren't you at Will's, Cy?"

Musing about it for several moments, Cy remarked, "Sal, if I didn't have a need to care for that house on my own, I might lose the will to care for myself. It animates my mind and body, so I labor daily. But a full house is the dream." Cy remembered building his green, two-room wooden house sixty years ago when he and Maggie married. On the porch swing, they clasped hands and felt that the whole world was theirs. They did this sitting and thinking after Cy's hard days at work for a few years. Then he bought Coon from an old friend, and life changed. One of them walked him daily, fed him, and he was like a child, helpless. Several times he was almost hit by cars before Cy built a fence in the back yard to keep him from the road. Cy had four more dogs named Coon, all hound dogs, over the next sixty years. After five years, Mark came into their lives.

From reading diligently, Mark's intelligence flourished, and he fantasized of being a doctor. Once he realized that the training required anatomy of deceased people, he recoiled. As he analyzed his dad doing detailed work with the blueprints of houses, he wanted to build them instead. So he volunteered to work for others after Cy taught him how to build most of a house. All over the city of Atlanta, he was sought until he got mugged, and after Will was born and became older, he was threatened by gangs. Then Will and his parents moved to Greentown, where Mark, Will's father, had met his wife, Jan, and fallen in love. With Cy, they rejoiced as a whole family again.

Darkness crept in, and Cy quivered about being alone. He dreaded night, when he felt those memories creep back in to drill his mind and send him back in time. Will rushed to Cy and blurted, "Hey Grandpa, you can't remain alone, so come to live with us tomorrow. Dad expects you to assist with a critical job, and he knows you're the specialist." Turning to leave, Cy was followed by Shannon and Sally, who bemoaned his failing to stay with them late as he usually did. Shannon boomed after him.

"Take it easy, Cy. If you get bored at work, you know where we are after school. Down by Slow Creek, the usual. As long as it's not flooding again," Shannon said, waving his Judy Blume book.

"You two study hard, and play no pranks on the teachers, okay? I recall some of the things done in my day. Many a frog was nearly sat upon, and there was always a misfit in the principal's office."

"Cy, I wish that's all we saw kids do, but these are harsher times. Often kids are expelled." Sally hung her head in shame at her own generation.

"Well Sal, that's serious. Someone should say that frogs

are okay to joke with but nothing else. Teachers really care about kids. I picked wildflowers for mine, and the ladies cheered it. But the few male teachers I had, well … Only got a quick grin from them."

"Gramps, Dad needs your skill to build one of those winding stairs you did for the governor years ago," Will interrupted.

"Okay, W," he said without thought. "In the morning I'll be over with my tools and jeans. You should try that flower idea, sometime, Sally and Shannon. Teachers like it. Plus, they remember it and forgive you quicker for minor wrongs. You can do many things for some people, but they please them more for some reason."

In Cy's mind, flowers were eternally in bloom, as they were love.

"Good idea, Cy; we'll try that," Shannon said and Sal agreed. "Most of us treasure flowers, and maybe it will make kids think outside themselves."

Sauntering up the street toward his green two-story house surrounded by pine, oak and two maple trees, Cy croaked, "Take care, all of you." Shannon and Sal headed home as well but waited until Cy trod to his place and plopped on his porch with his tool pouch slung over his shoulder. Trailing was old Coon, his long ears flapping as he galloped to catch his best friend. Cy was eager for tomorrow, as he polished each tool. Grinning, he had that twinkle in his eye that a guy who loves work gets.

Because they were living things, flowers are what Cy suggested. They granted more happiness than any old object given as a gift. It was something that came from the heart, and material items failed to do it. When he gave a lady a flower she'd blush and thank him by giving a big hug. He didn't get that when he gave them anything else. So he felt that flowers were somehow attached to the heart, and with each flower he gave his heart.

Whether it was a rose or a dandelion, the flower had a similar effect. When he was five years old, he brought plain weeds to his mother. Awed with appreciation, she couldn't explain the difference between plants of greater beauty and others that evinced only scowls of gardeners who sought them out as demons to be exorcised. Upon his sixth birthday, Cy was given a plant book and learned of the nuances between flowers and all other plants in the world. But to him dandelions were still flowers.

CHAPTER 3

Deciding to spend a final night in his house, Cy would savor it. Walking in, he let his mind meander and locked the door but not the deadbolt. He lay on the couch, and Coon slumped by his feet. The dog's eyes flickered several times, and then he slumbered. A wiggle of his ears told Cy he was still listening for prowlers.

As Cy drifted to sleep, he heard a knock at the door, then a staccato of knocks. Next, a gargantuan fist and arm smashed through the maple door. A foot slammed through where the door knob was. Through the door bounded seven-foot tall behemoth Flannery O'Conner who punted the couch, and Cy and the couch pounded the wall five feet away, exploding a gaping hole in it. Coon bared his teeth and barked, seeking an opportunity to leap at the intruder.

Shaking his head and flipping the couch back to the floor, Cy leaped at his former friend and slammed his fist into his stomach. Flannery didn't flinch. "Flan," Cy croaked, "we're going to hurt ourselves, but you don't burst my door and traumatize Coon." Cy swiped his left leg to the side of Flannery's left one and tripped him to the floor. Springing up, the big man had his say.

"McGinn, I never forgot that time you took my girlfriend. Then you married Maggie, my only love. Even if sixty years have passed, it's always in my mind and soul."

"Flan," Cy admitted, "she came to me; I didn't steal her. Your brain's too small for that big body. You know how it happened but don't want to remember. Yes, we'll settle it anyway, then it's over." Diving for the giant's legs, Cy rammed him against the table. The big man punched Cy in the face, Cy shook it off but spat some blood out of his mouth and his nose was bloody. Coon skittered between them and took Flannery off guard. Biting his leg, the dog bounded and snagged his stomach.

Flannery, crimson-faced and sweat pouring, swung his foot into Cy's chest. Cy gasped for breath and then slammed an elbow into Flannery's back, which knocked him to the floor. Struggling up on all fours, Flannery head butted Cy in his stomach. Cy in turn kneed him in the chin, snapping his head back so that he stumbled into the refrigerator. The door flew open, and jars tumbled out and shattered on the floor. Flannery slipped around on some mayonnaise and pounded onto his back again.

Cy crept to the phone but couldn't use it since Flannery had wrenched the cord from the wall. Rushing at Cy again, Flannery saw Cy snatch a lamp without a lampshade. He whipped it at Flannery's face and nipped his ear. The light bulb shattered and left the live filaments exposed, so that it electrocuted Flannery. He teetered while clutching his ear and scowled at Cy. Kicking at Coon, Flannery heard him yelp. Through the air Cy whisked with a kick to Flannery's chest and hammered him to the ground again. Flannery managed to hoist himself and crack his fist once more into Cy's face. Cy dropped against the embedded couch and onto its seat, flipping it upright. Flannery lunged for him and Cy dodged it, finally jacking his foot into Flannery's throat. Gasping for breath, Flannery stumbled backward onto the oak floor. Cy heard and saw the back of his head bang it.

He hung over Flannery as blood oozed from his nose and mouth onto Flannery's face, and from the rear of his skull, he saw blood trickle. "Now it is my problem," Cy groaned. "This will require a lawyer." Cy was six feet tall himself and muscles rippled in his arms. With shoulder length curly amber hair, his son, Mark, was five feet, ten inches tall. Jan, Mark's wife and Cy's daughter-in-law, was six feet, thin as a waif and sported horn-rimmed glasses only around other people for an image of intelligence.

Calling Mark with his sequestered room phone, Cy requested help. Mark answered, "Hey Dad, what's up? It's midnight."

"Son, call that lawyer, John Sebastian, to tell him I'm an offender. The old friend of mine, Flannery O'Conner, broke into the house, and we had a squall. You'd never know he's eighty. Strong as a bull. On the floor he lies, with a fractured skull. He may not be breathing. I'm afraid to check him. I'll call the police, expect trouble."

"Sure Dad, I'll call his night service, and he'll be there in a half hour. Let me know if you need me to come by. I'll be right there." Mark told Jan about the incident as she lounged on the edge of the bed next to him. Rolling her eyes, she sighed. Then she summoned Will and let him know. He sung the Scottish national anthem that Cy taught him. Trotting to the closet, he retrieved his own Scottish kilt and donned it. He rummaged for Cy's bagpipes and sang a rambunctious fight song. Cy heard that and wept, knowing that his family would be there for him. After listening several minutes, Cy moaned to Mark.

"I'll try to handle this myself but will call if I need you. Thanks, and try to get rest," he huffed. Then Cy hung up and called the police. Dialing 911, he reported the incident. "This is Cy McGinn, and I've had a break-in. The guy who assaulted me is injured with a skull fracture."

The dispatcher said, "We'll send an officer right away. Are you at 112 Klaus Street, sir?" she inquired.

"That's it," Cy stated. "I'll be waiting but hope the intruder makes it."

"Then we're sending emergency medical service, too. Keep calm and an eye on the man. Observe any changes of stopped breathing, okay?"

"Right, glad he's going to get medical attention. He was a good friend."

"I'm sorry to hear that. We'll do all we can for him. They should be there in ten minutes." She slammed her phone down.

Cy plopped in his easy chair and petted Coon, saying, "Old boy, if you could talk, I'd be out of this mess fast. But you can't, so at least give me comfort." Yawning, Coon lay resolutely at Cy's feet. In fifteen minutes, Cy heard a voice boom through the doorway.

"Inspector McGeever, here;" he snapped. Eyeing Cy and then the prostrate body of Flannery, he muttered, "He's not so well, but I hope that though you're busted up, you're well, Mr. McGinn," and he kneeled to finger the downed man's wound. "Look's like a fracture, no doubt. Oh, here's the EMS," he said as he pivoted to the doorway. "Come in and check him out," McGeever said, as he gestured to the body on the floor.

Donning their rubber gloves, the EMS crew gently picked up Flannery's head to examine his skull. "Yep, it's a skull fracture. It looks like Mr. McGinn will have to make a statement," one of the men grunted. There were two men and a woman, all with powerful arms and legs and about six feet tall. Their uniforms were crisp, neat and said 'Greentown EMS' on them.

"Wait a moment;" another tech paused, coursing her hand across the throat of Flannery. "Looks like his esophagus is partially damaged, too. Let me check for a pulse and breathing." Doing so, she pronounced him barely alive. "Get the oxygen and saline IV in here stat! Let me check his heart." She passed her hand to his chest. "Heart has stopped. Bring the paddles."

So two other techs brought the IV bags and the cardiac defibrillator machine. They hooked each IV up, and the tech kneeling on the floor placed the paddles on Flannery's chest. A pop and a jerk of the body. Still nothing. He tried two more times, then checked for a heartbeat. "Ah, we have him back," he smiled. "Get the monitor for him until we get him to the emergency room." She brought it in.

Rolling the stretcher in, all three lowered it, then picked up Flannery and slid him onto it. They rolled him out to the truck, shoved him in the rear, entered the truck themselves, flipped on the flashing white and purple lights and siren and drove off.

Dressed in a cashmere jacket, Gucci shoes and tailored grey pants, a man slithered through the doorway and strode toward Cy. At barely five feet tall, with dark brown eyes and partially balding, he didn't look like much of a lawyer. But his thundering voice offered Cy the sense of power that he sought in the profession. He extended his hand and said, "Mr. McGinn, you're entitled to silence as Inspector uh … "

"Inspector McGeever, for the record," McGeever said, refusing to shake the lawyer's hand as he drilled a cigarette into his pursed lips.

"Yes, I'll answer the questions, and all responses go through me, Inspector. I'm Mr. McGinn's attorney, John Sebastian. Nice to meet you," and he nodded his head toward him in respect.

"I'm charging Mr. McGinn with assault until proven otherwise. So we'll meet you at the station." To no avail, Coon hung his head and howled. McGeever clamped the handcuffs on Cy's wrists in front of him so they bit into them, and he began to bleed. Snatching him by the neck, the inspector forced Cy out the doorway. He jerked open the rear door of the police car and shoved him onto the seat, then entered the driver's side, gunned the engine and drove off.

Securing what was left of the door behind him, John hustled to his Maserati, entered it, started it and raced to catch the inspector. He sped to 80 miles per hour in three seconds, and a mile down the road pulled behind him, tailing him to the station. When they both arrived and stopped, all exited the cars. John said, "Watch it, Inspector; you may have a police brutality charge on your hands."

"We'll see about that," he growled at John and scowled. "Come on McGinn; into the station we go," he bellowed and again abused Cy, dragging him through the station door to the booking station.

Entering through the front doors, John depressed the call button on the wall and said, "I'm here as Cyrus

McGinn's lawyer and need to see him as soon as he's processed."

"No problem," the voice on the other end muttered. "We'll send an officer for you when we're done."

"Thanks," he grunted. He lounged on the crude oak bench, scrawling notes on the case and evidence as he waited. In an hour, a portly police officer with dragons tattooed on his arms waddled out to meet him and usher him to the jail holding cell area.

"Come on, Mr. Sebastian," the officer said. He knew John well because of his many night calls. "Mr. McGinn is in cell number three. Help yourself to him."

"We won't be long," John responded. The officer tipped his hat in response. Walking to Cy's cell, John called to him. He had already laid down on the rigid cot they called a bed and was alone.

Cy had not been near a jail and never would be again. His driving record was even perfect for sixty-four years. Being a good, law-abiding citizen, he was in the wrong place at the wrong time. Behind him, he glared at the empty cot and imagined he saw legions that had been in the same situation he was, had really done nothing except defend themselves and their property. Seeing it differently, the law said that anything they felt was committed someone had to answer for, and this time is was Cyrus McGinn who had to say why.

"John, hope you can arrange bail right now, as I've got to get back to my dog," Cy pleaded as he stood up and shuffled to the bars. He spun his massive hands through the bars, clutched John's collar and jerked him to the cruel steel of his cage, then let go. He stood back and stuttered, "I'm sorry. Forgive me, as I'm nervous and scared."

"Cy, Mark sent me, and you should be out in an hour.

I'm on retainer, so I'll pay the bond, and I'll drive you home." He waved his hand to flip his collar back in place.

"What about a court date?" Cy whispered.

"Don't worry; I've never lost a case. I'll go to court in absentia, or in your absence. If you need to show up, I'll call you. But we'll get it dismissed," John boasted. "Hold on a bit, okay?" Swallowing a grin, he shook Cy's powerful hands through the bars. "You're innocent. Breaking into your home, a man assaulted you and your dog and could have killed you. It happens to thousands throughout the country. We'll say our prayers."

"Sure," Cy said. "What else can I do?" he asked, shrugged his shoulders and wept.

John trod back out to the waiting area and paced. In a little over an hour, the bailiff came to let Cy out. Walking out to the waiting area, he told John, "Let's go. I never want to see this again." They marched to John's car and got in. John started it and the five-hundred horsepower engine rumbled to life. "It's nothing like my Packard," Cy cooed. "You legal guys sure know how to pick your wheels." His eyes twinkled and he sighed.

"It took me ten years of sweating small cases to win the big ones that got me this," John said. "I'm single, so this is my toy, and on the track I've had it up to 160 once in a while." He whistled the U.S. Air Force fight song.

"That's okay, I won't challenge you to a duel," Cy cracked. Glancing at the dials on the instrument panel, he said, "Sure wouldn't mind driving it sometime" and drooled.

"Here, give it a spin," John said, skidding over to the curb. "Get on the interstate, though." So Cy and he changed seats, Cy revved up and flew up the road to the first interstate entrance ramp. The trunk lid popped up, the lock broken due to the stress.

"Yes sir, this machine will do tricks," he squealed as he rocketed to 70 in only a few seconds. The car felt like it sailed over the road, not on it. Passing a tractor-trailer, Cy heard the driver honk the horn in approval. The yellow dynamo reached the exit to Cy's house, and he smoked the brakes when he slowed down.

Veering off the ramp, he squealed the tires a few times on the way to his house. Reaching the driveway, he parked at the curb and cut the engine off. He and John got out, and he asked John if he'd be okay with the broken trunk lid. "Sure," John said. "I'm not one to think that I'll have a problem twice in one night. Okay, then, Cy, take care, and if you need me anymore, you call me next time. You can handle my car; I'll handle you." With a smirk he shook Cy's hand and waved while he briskly strode to his car. He slid in, revved up and rumbled down the road out of sight.

"What a guy," cackled Cy as he stumbled up his driveway and opened his broken door. He walked over to Coon, petted him a few times and shoved the couch back from the wall. He closed the door as well as he could and said, "Now it's almost home sweet home. Good night buddy." Then he pounced on the couch to slumber quickly.

CHAPTER 4

As the morning sun shone through the window, Cy woke up, swigged his cup of coffee and called the locksmith. He told him to be there in an hour and went to the Greentown Hardware and More to buy another door that might fit. Taking it home, he shaved the edges with a saw but finally got it to mesh. Then the locksmith came, reworked the lock and left.

Cy squeezed out the door, locked it and walked to Mark's house with his tool pack. He tapped on Mark's door and rang the doorbell as Mark, Will's dad, answered. Opening the door, Mark hugged him. "Glad you made it, Dad. After beating the biggest man in town, you can fight for me now. Just kidding," Mark swallowed a grin. "Come on in, though, and relax before we go to work." Mark and Jan had a two-story split-level house with one room upstairs and two down. For fifteen years they had owned it, since Maggie died, and they knew that Cy would want them there. When they had moved from Atlanta, Will took karate, two classes a week, in case he was harassed by any thugs again.

"Hey there, Pop. Make yourself at home. Jan is almost done making sandwiches. Due to an unexpected last-minute meeting at work yesterday, she started a little late. As much as I try to keep up with her, it's a losing battle." Mark walked with a strut that he learned in military school. Being generous, he would give the shirt off of his back to one in need.

Vivacious and seldom needing much rest, Jan had brown deer eyes, and the silky long blond hair to her waist is what had attracted Mark to her. Plus, her personality was strong, so no one tried to abuse her emotionally or physically. She was Irish and could fight as well as the Scottish. Holding her temper, she instead used her bright mind to work where she did. As a supervisor, she had to hire and fire but gave those fired a second chance after several months. She believed in forgiveness.

"No problem, Mark," Cy said. "I only need to make sure that Coon gets a dish of chow. He's having a rough time with his tummy. Guess it's like us, getting older has its own rewards and problems." At that, Coon hopped up on the couch to watch an old episode of "Lassie" on TV.

"Gramps, come here and look at this bird on the tree limb. What is it?" Will piped. Bounding to the window, Cy eyed a small bird flitting by near it. "I think it's a chickadee, W, and it looks like a flock of them." Instantly the whole tree churned with chirping and hopping birds. "Must be gathering for that winter flight south, as they sure are busy finding out who's in charge."

"Coon is going crazy pacing that window," Will stammered.

"It's amazing how he won't bark, though. Seeing so many, he gets confused and can't figure out what in the world to do. Some hunter," Cy cracked, wagging his head as he scratched his ear.

"Good thing he can't catch them!" Will exclaimed. "If one pecked him on the nose, he'd really yelp." He snickered and poked his own nose in imitation.

"Yeah, once it happened when he scared a momma too close to the nest," Cy said.

"He sticks to chasing squirrels now and runs like a nut when they chase in return," Will returned.

"Okay, enough conversation. Time for you to head out the door for school, W, and we have to get going," Cy said.

"Righty, Gramps. Have a good one," Will said with a bow and dashed out the door.

Jan handed Cy and Mark the lunch cooler, kissed Mark, and bid them out as well, then finished her own work to leave.

CHAPTER 5

One day Coon erred. A squirrel baby was in the yard and he caught it. As he bit it, it snapped him, and he howled. Will saw it and hurtled out to notice the dog's bleeding muzzle. He screamed, "Hey Coon, we're going to the vet." Dragging the dog by the collar, Will struggled to the door and burst into the house. "Mom, Dad, Coon was bitten by a squirrel and may have gotten rabies." The dog swiped his paw against the wound and then licked it repeatedly.

"Let me see, boy," Mark said, clenching Coon's jaw. "Yep, we're going right now. Jan, we're going to Dr. Erasmus' office."

"Okay," she boomed from upstairs. "See you later." In anxiety, she quivered and scratched.

Mark and Will went to the truck with Coon on a leash and put him between them. "Keep calm, buddy; we'll help you," Will moaned. After driving five miles to the office, they got out of the truck and led Coon in.

"We need to see Dr. Erasmus. Coon was bitten by a squirrel," Mark told Wendy, the vet assistant.

"Okay. He'll be out in fifteen minutes. Oh, that is a nasty wound," she said to Coon. She grabbed a petri dish, then opened a cotton swab and swept it over the wound and over the medium to take a culture for infection.

It was thirty minutes, but Dr. Erasmus came out, checked Coon and stated, "For wild animal bites, we have to quarantine him for ten days. Sorry, Mark."

"Okay, it's better than us getting rabies," Mark blubbered.

"If there are any rabies symptoms we'll call you. If so, he'll have to be euthanized. In the meantime, we give him antibiotics unless a negative culture precludes it." He gently tilted Coon's head up and eyed the wound, then sighed.

"Oh no, Gramps wouldn't go for that," Will stammered.

"It's law, Will. We couldn't help it," said Dr. Erasmus.

"Well okay, here he is," Mark said, and Dr. Erasmus walked Coon to a holding cage.

"See you later, friend." Will wept as he went out to the truck. Walking out, Mark got in the truck, while Will slumped into his seat and closed the door.

Rabies was a frightening disease. To an animal, it meant death, whether by the disease itself or by euthanasia if it were taken to the vet. A pet had to be kept from wild animals, but doing that to extreme would make it a prisoner of the house. When they ushered him to the back yard, Cy, Jan and Mark had always eyed Coon, but it only takes a second for a wild animal to attack. Even with his rabies vaccination, he still had to be observed by a vet, as there was no guarantee he wouldn't get the disease anyway. Squirrels were rampant, so it was bound to happen when he continued the chase. If he had stuck with threatening birds, Coon might have had an eye pecked out, but wouldn't get rabies. He meant too much to Cy to go that way and might see old age.

"Chances are that he's okay, Will. Don't worry about it unless we get a call," Mark groaned.

"Sure, got it Dad. Hope they don't kill him." Will's head drooped.

"He'll make it," Mark said, sighing in desperation.

They went home and broke the news to Jan and Cy. When euthanasia was mentioned they both squirmed. "He'll come through; always has," Cy said. Then he went to his room and laid down.

After ten days, Dr. Erasmus called to report that Coon was free of rabies. "You can pick him up now. But keep him indoors for awhile, except for normal needs. From now on, watch him while he plays."

"Sure," Mark whispered into the phone. "Thanks, Doc," and he hung up. "Good news all. There's no rabies, but we don't let Coon out of sight in the back yard. Except for his duty, he remains indoors two weeks. Doc said it." Mark, Cy and Will went to retrieve Coon. Looking depressed, he still sensed it was to his benefit as they voiced his restriction. When they arrived home, Coon hopped up on Will's bed to take a nap. The McGinns chuckled in relief.

"Gramps, Coon loves people more than hunting. Too bad he can't find a buddy to go to dog school with. It would be the best thing for him," Will said. To adjust to the new routine, Coon took several months. Eying squirrels warily, he avoided them when he was out. Cy and Will walked him often, and he yearned for that. Upon returning, he panted, exhausted. Then, when he napped, he'd shiver as if having nightmares. To calm him down, someone stroked him. He awakened to lap the hand of the person who gentled his mind. His usual routine was thwarted by his anxiety, and a few times he had to be cradled for ten minutes or so to allow him to function normally. But he'd come out of it.

CHAPTER 6

In the kitchen one day a fire exploded when Jan forgot and left something on the stove. Coon woke up to smell the smoke, leaped at everyone and barked, then pranced to the kitchen and barked again. Noticing it first, Jan blurted, "Oh my, look what I did by leaving." Mark and Cy snatched the fire extinguisher, lunged at the fire and spewed the whole stove with the contents. Believing these were things that befell people who weren't as moral, they felt that they had erred for it to happen. After the fire was out, they all prayed that they would be safe from harm from now on and thanked God for all of the blessings of their lives and each day after. When it was calmer, Jan decided that they would still try to eat.

"Okay all. Time to sit around the campfire and roast some wieners and marshmallows," Jan joked, placing the last glass on the table. Eying the pot carrying the chicken, last item, to the table, Coon lay by the chair that Cy always sat at.

They agreed that Mark would say the grace, and after he said thanks for everyone, he offered Cy the first bit of food. As usual, he took his portion last and assured everyone was happy. Before Mark ate, he scratched Coon behind the ears.

"So we have to put that staircase into Dr. McKenzie's new house, and he wants the oak banister in case his kids decide to take a slide ride down it?" asked Cy with his normal sly humor.

He thought about how he had made a swing set for Mark when he was a child and then made one for Will also as he got old enough to play on one. To keep them occupied, he also carved them crafts such as the wooden wagons that they pulled their dogs in with their tricycles. Also, there were tree houses and forts where they pretended they were in the western days and scanned for Indians.

"Then there are the wooden animals with wheels Doctor McKenzie had crafted for his twins. They rode them until they fell apart," Will said. "But he really loves those kids and sacrifices for them. They aren't spoiled, though, and he teaches them to respect others."

"I hear that the twins are in Will's class, right Will?" asked Jan.

"Yes, Mom, but they aren't doted on. Because she feels their dad prefers it, Mrs. Smith works them more than the rest of the class. They're pleasant, though, and aren't arrogant. They only answer yes and no ma'am."

"That's great that the doctor is making sure they're sociable. Everyone needs friends, including them. Kids whose parents have money might feel uneasy in schools when they are treated differently," Jan observed.

"We're going to have a fine time on that house," Cy interrupted. "It's cheers that we're going to have a good family moving in it when it's done, and I rejoice to think about it. Even my tools glow in their pouch."

"Gramps, each time you think about wood, I see your face shine. It's no wonder those trees are in your yard. They remind you of your favorite things to do, saw and hammer," Will added.

"Well, Will, it's the days it takes to make that curved hand railing that intrigue me. They're like a long snake and you have to handle a little at a time, as a real python. If you fail to use caution, it gets away from you as well," advised Cy.

"Yeah, those ten-year-old twins give Doc a go some days. I was told that the tree swing with those strong ropes lasted only a few months. Playing on it so much made the ropes thin out on it that fast. But in an hour a better one was up. That boy and girl are the love of his life and his wife's pride as well," Mark admitted.

CHAPTER 7

Cy knew that the wealthy don't have it nearly as harsh in some parts of life as others. Then he envisioned those children going places and doing things that his family could never go. He didn't envy them as much as he knew what Mark, Jan and Will had missed out on. Dwelling upon it so that things he lost stuck in his heart, he mourned. Mark was taught everything that Cy knew so that he'd do well later. But Cy realized that they would only rise so high, and they would have to be content with life, what they had. It troubled them to think that way, but after a while, they did it easily.

"Dad, I know it was that hands-on stuff you showed me when I was young that made me what I am. It was years ago, when I was a boy, but my mind still remembers the first of those snake railings we built. It was summer, and a friend had invited me to the beach. Somehow I sensed the water could wait so that I finished what I started," Mark said.

"That reminds me, Dad, that I have to work on that birdhouse that I began a few weeks ago. Guess that I goofed off and let it set in the closet too long. I've painted two sides and half of the roof. So that leaves about half," said Will.

"One of these days, Gramps and Dad can allow you to work on a big house, Will. But I trust that you'll get into college so you can operate that firm Gramps started in. Then maybe you can have your own someday. Remember Buckminister Fuller who created that geodesic dome? Wouldn't be so many indoor football games, music concerts or other events if not for that," Jan spouted.

Cy knew she was talking about something that was out of his league. As an architect, he still couldn't create to the level of someone like Buckminister Fuller. To have him for a positive influence was worthy, but he and Mark did pleasing, normal work. When they finished a job, they were proud of it, and others were, too. Building is not always celebrated, so the world knows you by name, but it is a feeling of accomplishment that is unknown in many other jobs. It's getting it done and done right.

"Dad, I know you were an architect, and a lot of what you did was on paper, but it makes you feel accomplished each step of the way, like writing a hit song or bestseller," Mark said.

"Hey Dad, that makes me think. We've got a choir try-out next week, and I know that I can make it. Mrs. Smith said that she walked by the auditorium and heard me performing the minor singing part in the play last month. She talked to the drama teacher and wants me in that class. To put my heart on the line is what I love. Look at Clay Aiken.

He wasn't real attractive when he began, either," chirped Will.

Being a singer or song artist, Will knew, and making it onto a record label would take years of hard work. His grandfather had tried and given up on it, so he was expecting a challenge. But he would persevere, and maybe he'd be one of the lucky ones who became a success at what he loved to do. To make it, he realized Mrs. Smith was the first key. Being a music teacher, she knew what it took to get to the top. She had performed herself on Broadway but instead wanted to teach after several years. What was given to her was returned to the world.

"Right, W. It's how badly someone wants something, and he or she has to keep believing in the skill. Constant practice, love of the art, study and taking every opportunity to show their talents to others, especially those who can move them ahead in life, in this case, the music directors, producers and artist and repertoire people is needed," said Cy.

It was a constant learning process, which Cy took to, but he realized that he was limited on the energy that he had. He knew that it was always something that he had to work at, thinking about it until he felt it was right in his mind and heart.

Practicing techniques so he would get it right, he would take them home. This wasn't what he wanted, but realizing that he couldn't do much else, he told himself that he would need to do it and not complain about it. There were times when he really saw and knew that it was going to be a long road and finally understood the truth of it; if he wanted to be happy, he had to work at that, too. So he smiled and did so.

How did you learn all that, Dad?" inquired Mark. "Have

you been watching 'American Idol,' or did you do some work in the field? You really know the lingo."

"About fifty years ago. It started when I was drawing plans for a recording studio in Nashville. Someone had done a little work with Elvis and offered to teach me how to run one of those outfits. Once, I shook hands with Elvis, and he took a liking to me as well. He let me meet his new girlfriend Priss. She and he were married later, of course. In the few sessions I took part, they flipped when I picked it all up like a pro. During the year I spent there it became one of RCA's major studios. Elvis did most of his work there. In all areas of music, big names are doing CD's there now."

"Wow, you mean you were kind of famous but didn't want to do that for the rest of your life. You could have recorded me when I get good enough to do back-up for Clay Aiken," Will moaned.

"W, I was going to stay in that same studio since Elvis wanted me on, but it was Colonel Parker, who ran the show, who kept me out of there. Sometimes he was a good guy, but he was in charge and couldn't even take someone in the studio with him on the final take of a song," said Cy. "That was just the way it was."

He knew that Elvis was famous from the fifties through the early seventies and that he might not do so well once the Beatles really came along and gained popularity. So, biding his time, he thought about his architect skills. Putting them to use, he did the accounting for his company as well, finally doing it most of the time. Elvis was the 'king' of rock and roll for his day, but he would be gone by the seventies, and Cy didn't know it then. Something told him to keep his regular job he learned in college, so he did. Then he would be able to take care of Maggie and, later, Mark.

"Well Cy, it's a long way from fame and fortune in Music City to tapping nails in Greentown. Don't you miss the opportunity, all the interesting people and world travel that were part of that life?" mused Jan. "It would still be bugging me when it was years later. Getting older I'd still be thinking of it, even your age if it happened to me." She knew it would have meant he may not have had a family or maybe Mark. So her life would have been entirely different and not as happy. In one way or another, she realized that Cy would be there and add to the family. One of the ways was the love and care he would give, and that would always be there. Cy was a kid at heart and thought like one; he needed family around him for support. Without them, he really felt despair that was difficult to eliminate.

"Of course I'd like to be there. It was long and odd hours, sometimes sixteen or maybe more at a time. You would be so tired that you could only sit or lay. Cherishing every moment, you felt time stood still, and any problem drifted off with that song, the voice and artist behind the mike. No matter whether it's their first song or fifty-first, it comes from the heart, and it's all special." Hanging his head and gazing at the floor, he was lost in the past for a few moments. "I wish Elvis were still here, singing with his silver and white rhinestone suit. In most ways he was a good man, but his fans became his life, mainly the reason why he sang and performed. He didn't separate the two, and that's what happened to him. In the music and acting fields that is more likely to happen. Those people often love their jobs the most and get benefits out of it that money can buy, like houses, land, horses and beauty."

More and more Cy thought about his past, the mirth he had recording, being with Elvis and knowing that Maggie was really the first love of his life. Around her clouds disappeared, and the sun eternally shone. Oh, they argued at times but worked it out so they stayed together. She was there with him at the long recording sessions, but he felt guilty. At times he knew that he was going to sing and be the one with the golden voice. But he realized how stressful it was on Elvis. Thousands of people in his audience desired to be pleased, not only the people he recorded for. Cy saw him journey the world, not only in the U.S., and the crowds cheered, did anything to show Elvis they loved him. He, in turn, expressed love to them. That is what drove him to the edge and finally cost him his life. He couldn't love his fans back enough, or so he thought.

CHAPTER 8

"What do you think about music now, Dad?" Mark inquired. "Do people really listen to songs because of the person singing or the music behind it?"

"It's usually the lyrics, Mark. That's the song. There can be a good tune, but the words are why people buy it. That's why Elton John has one person whom he trusts and who has written most of his songs for his musical life. It's a perfect match and always will be. Elton's the perfect performer for those songs. Often it's the lead singer in groups who writes or helps write the songs, such as Paul McCartney and John Lennon of the Beatles and Brian Wilson of the Beach Boys."

"Okay, anyone for hitting the hay?" suggested Will. "My choir tryout is tomorrow, and I'll need rest to make my voice the best. Mrs. Smith is selective about her performers. Red eye is not something that she tolerates, either. She says that the world is your stage, but you have to earn the rewards from it."

"Good way to put it, Will. If we're creative people, we all have to earn respect or fans. Nobody gives you a following. In any other field, that doesn't apply," said Jan.

"I forgot that I need to study the lyrics for the program, a set of songs for a major musical play we'll be doing. I think it's 'South Pacific' by Rogers and Hammerstein," said Will.

"That's fantastic, Will. It'll remind your mom and me of our honeymoon in Hawaii," Mark said. "We'll see the rehearsals and the play. You know, when it was cast as a movie, it was so well done. The cast and story are some of the best there are."

"It was an adventure to remember, for sure," cracked Jan. "That coconut barely missed me. Then I noticed other coconuts falling, and it was a hazardous spot." She thought of coconuts as stones, and if they fell on your head, they did a lot of damage. As you walked along one could fall from the tree and pop your noggin, knocking you out or damaging your brain, a small but possible risk. "I especially remember that one plummeted from the tree and almost struck your head. To gather the rest, you fumbled to climb it. After a few feet, you plopped on the sand. Finally shimmying up it and grabbing them, a beach boy brought them to us as a late wedding gift."

"During lessons, that hula skirt almost slipped off you, so the teacher blushed and tossed a towel over you," said Mark, hiding a grin. "It was right before a luau, and everyone had a great meal because of it."

"I was able to go there when they filmed 'Blue Hawaii' with Elvis," added Cy. "Some see it as an American paradise, but too costly to live there. Guess it's seems lonely and so far out, is why. After years, some people who move there leave, and others may stay. To have sun all year, palm trees, ocean and some mountains is a dream for many. There are all kinds of birds, and so many races of people make it unlikely that one will get bored by old ideas." He soaked in not only sun but also culture while there.

"Well, maybe we can all take a trip there if we can put a little money aside and look ahead to next summer," Mark suggested. "We can learn how to surf and understand one of the major island ways of life. Also, we can learn how to use an outrigger canoe."

"If I go, I won't have to wear one of those flower necklaces, I hope," said Will, blushing. "Looking at flowers I love but not to be stared at by people on the beach."

"Oh Will," Jan responded. "Only when you ask them do they do that. Not everyone gets them. They're called leis, and they're often at the airport when you first arrive to encourage friendship between visitors and the people who live there."

"Okay, I'll go then. Maybe I can be taught to climb a coconut tree," said Will.

"We can go hiking, as that's one of the more natural activities, seeing a new place and being with other people. There are mountain paths, waterfalls and wild woods with lots of green," Mark said. He felt they had a good home, but visiting other places was invigorating.

None of them knew the risks or the joys that the islands held. There have been volcanic eruptions on the Big Island, attacks against tourists on all islands and hurricanes. It is truly a paradise with perils. Enjoy but with caution and awareness.

CHAPTER 9

"With the right planning we can relish much. It's critical to create multiple ideas beforehand so that when we arrive, we can make the best of it. We'll scrutinize tour guides and talk about it." Cy's ears wiggled and eyebrows twitched with anticipation.

Hawaii is unique in the U.S. It's the only South Pacific island state in the country. Hawaiians feel the islands were stolen from them, and they want them back, so they've been angry. Millions of tourists invade annually anyway to feel the trade winds, see the native Hawaiians and how they'd live, if others weren't there. It's flowery, green and has two volcanoes, one occasionally erupting.

"We can all use more exhilaration, and it begins with Cy spending more time here. An addition to Will's room built by Mark has a drawing table, lamp, books, radio and telephone. There's a mammoth walk-in closet for clothes, tools and toys," said Jan.

"Sounds intriguing to me," said Cy. "Old Coon needs a change for a time, and I know Will entertains him with chase. Plus he has a knack for scratching his ears in a perfect way." He was wary of vacating his house after the break-in, so would check it daily.

With that, Coon scampered up and down the hallway and growled approval at everyone each time he reached the table and turned about again. When he was snappy, it was obvious that Cy was too.

"I'm headed to the shower. It was a bit warm today, and we were sweating a rainstorm. Whoever needs to can follow me," Mark said.

"That reminds me to give Coon a bath this weekend," Cy added. "It's not his favorite activity, but he's going anyway." About then, the dog crawled under Will's bed so fast that the dust balls flew up to collect on the desk. He found a stray spider and nibbled it.

"That's okay, Coon. I'm not one to like a bath, either, right Mom?" Will scraped a dab of mud from his shoe and smeared his face.

Jan admitted, "Yes, you and Coon have that in common, staying from soap and water. Rather than spend fifteen minutes getting clean, you want to tumble in a dirt mound all day."

"That's because outside bests inside most of the time, except as Gramps found, when the lightning strikes," and Will wriggled his eyebrows.

"Cy, are you still trying to set yourself on fire?" Jan asked with a giggle. "Smokey the Bear will toss dirt at you if any of his trees burn down due to your foolishness."

"You know that I've had that head plate so long it's like my teeth. Until it's used, I'm unaware it's there. In this case, my head was a lightning bolt catcher."

"I'm glad you wear that old hat, though. It's a lot better for you when a storm comes," Jan snickered.

"Yeah, don't know what farmer created them, but sunburn is only inconvenient compared to getting zapped. Instead of feeling that tingling skin when it's coming like they say will happen, I hear a whistling like a whippoorwill. Then when I'm looking for a bird, pop goes the cork! I ought to have my head wired to the Weather Channel," Cy quipped.

In actuality, he knew that in an instant he may have been in the afterlife. Lightning was deadly to a number of people annually, and he'd scramble for shelter at the next storm. You don't tempt fate. He was only alive now because he never did so. The wise know the limits of reality and seldom attempt to exceed them. Risk is amusing, but only intelligent risk is what the average person engages in.

CHAPTER 10

Mark had seconds ago entered the shower when Coon straggled in. "Coon, you can't share the shower," Mark moaned. He had bumped his head into the wall, then into the toilet and the cabinets before finally ambling toward the shower where he popped the partly latched bathroom door and hopped into the shower stall. Onto the floor splashed water, creating a shallow reflecting pool. Coon then stood, eyed his reflection, growled and bared his teeth at the opponent. As rapidly as he could, he then lapped the spill.

"Good guy, buddy. If you hadn't cleaned up, you'd have slept outside tonight. Jan keeps this place perfect." Luckily only his feet were wet, and he darted out unseen. Then he crept to Will's bed and laid at the foot of it, as he closed one eye and kept watch with the other while Will studied.

"Hey Coon, help me keep time with the chorus in this song," Will said. "Tap your front paw every so often." And sure enough, he did, as if he heard the drumbeats through the headphones Will wore as he repeated the lyrics with the CD. Coon even bobbed his head at the same time. "You've really got the rhythm. Maybe you could be on 'America's Funniest Home Videos.' Perhaps I can see if Mrs. Smith will have you sit in on rehearsals and keep us focused," Will said. Putting one paw over each ear, Coon growled at the suggestion. He shied from public view, obviously not star struck.

"He really loves it here, and I can already tell that Coon is ready for another house and another family. At home he was never that playful," Cy said. "He's still young enough, like any kid, to need various people around to keep him involved. Boredom is not any better for him than it is for us. What drives him is play like work keeps us going. But the best for him would be a friend of his own kind. If one of us could walk him every day, we'd have a better chance at it."

Coon trampled obstacles. Being a strong dog of a hundred pounds, he had climbed mountains, swam in the ocean and made it across a lake over a half-mile wide. Upon going north one winter, his instinct told him there was someone caught in a blizzard. She had been buried and almost frozen below three feet of snow. Finding her, he earned a hero medal from the mayor in Michigan where he was. He was then invited to be in the Christmas parade and to stay for a New Year's celebration. Upon arrival back in Greentown, Mayor Primo made a major affair of it. He requested Coon's picture in the paper and told people he was a citizen of valor. At a special ceremony Coon even smiled, which he had rarely done, and pranced up on stage.

"Great idea," said Jan. "All the time I see people at the park, and some even said that their dog looks forward to meeting other ones. He or she helps them acquire new friends, and on weekends the park has become the place to be."

"That walking them with a bicycle is good, too. To both of you it gives variety and you go farther than both walking, so the whole town is in your hands," Cy said. "Plus in the summer you stay cooler, if you miss the winter."

"Just take a helmet to help you in case you have a tumble," Jan said. "Not everyone is as coordinated as Lance Armstrong, and all pros wear them."

"Oh, I have that orange one that the fire department gave me. On it is bright reflective tape to be seen at night. Then when I add a flasher, I'm a real rainbow," chuckled Cy. "But people driving always see me and respect me."

"It wouldn't help much to see Coon, though," Jan said. "He likes the grass when he walks, too. Never did like the road."

"You have a point. Better go daytime if I'm going to use the bike. At night we can stay on the sidewalk." He wasn't going to be the first bike casualty.

"That way, he can enjoy sniffing the grass and bushes as he loves to do. To get him going, there are enough trees that a squirrel may even scurry by."

"In that case, I'm going to have to put an iron grip on the handle to keep him from racing. Of course, he'll try to drag me if I don't agree, as usual. If he had more fur, he could be an Alaskan sled hound. I'm sure that I can pedal as fast as he can run, so we'll be good competition."

"Coon might even qualify to be one of those rescue dog members. He's intelligent, obedient and a hard worker. We could find out if he could do that part-time, at least. If they wanted him more often, you'd have to approve it."

"Hey, now you're talking. That would be a great way for

him to earn his keep every so often. Plus I could know that maybe we contributed to saving lives. He'd learn a lot, and that would give him a real purpose to his days. Outside of their families, very few animals do that."

"All over, even worldwide, they need them, so he may get to travel some as well. Whenever any disaster happens, they can go to work to save people."

"Oh, that would be perfect for him. Thinking about travel, he acts as if life is cheers. If he could go somewhere all day, non-stop, it would be a dream job. Looks like my manner rubbed off on him in a most positive way," said Cy.

Coon snorted at everyone when they spoke of him in a whirlwind job. It was almost like he was smiling, but he opened his mouth and yawned. Shuffling in circles, he looked like he was chasing his tail. But he was seeking the best place to lie down. His ears quivered up and down, so Cy could tell that he was listening. Rescuing Cy and Maggie so often from trouble made it certain he'd cater to others, too. He might dislike it as a sled dog, since he shivered whenever he went to a cold place and would bound up to the first house he saw and scratch at the door to be let inside.

CHAPTER 11

"Tell me about some of your travels you had in the Packard," Jan begged. "I recall that a story about you was in the New York Times on being the first person to see all fifty states on the new interstate. That was a lot of driving back then." Not only was it driving but negotiating a gauntlet of new signs, numbers and directions that could be confusing.

Traveling at much higher speeds made vehicles more dangerous, especially before seatbelts. Cy and Maggie had to flick their eyes to see any sights still there. On the sides of the roads were big boards that jutted up from the ground and spouted messages. They saw ads like, "visit Al's diner and be a ham," "see caverns where mice fear to go," "eat a lot and gain a lot," "swim here in summer and ice fish in winter," "see you when the cow jumps over the moon," and "don't need an alarm, rooster wakes the farm."

"That's right. Guess that was my fifteen minutes of fame, as the pop artist Andy Warhol called it. It meant months of speeches all over this grand land," Cy said. "President Eisenhower was so smitten that he invited Maggie and me to the White House with all the trimmings. But hold on. Talking about that later when we may have more time is best, on a holiday, perhaps."

"Sure, Cy. To listen to those tales later, guess we should all get some shut eye. Besides, Will has a fit if he misses any of your stories. In his eyes, he gets a starry look that says he can't get enough of your past," Jan admitted.

"Jan, it's been said for years, 'those who don't learn from history are destined to repeat it.' But I must add, if you don't know about the past, the future has no purpose and the present has no place. Things have moved too fast, and the earthquakes and tsunamis are meant to slow us down." He trembled in fear as he said that.

"Stopping to smell the roses, you mean. That's an old saying, too, but for all of us it has so much meaning." She also knew that you had to keep your nose out of the thorns when you did so, the thorns being the trouble that can hide within the beauty of life.

"And look around at all the gifts we've been given. Birds, trees, flowers, tigers, elephants, fish and the oceans, clouds and storms. It's all the biggest and the best motion picture in the universe. With all their high-tech robotic electronic wizardry, Hollywood can't touch that. In comparison, those are all only drums in the distance," Cy observed. "As long as I've been around, the everyday wonders are what make us human and allow us to touch the face of God." Saying this, he felt his face become ashen, his feet pattered the floor, and a bright ring of light, flaming like a sun, encircled his head. Then as quickly as it shone, it was gone.

"That's the oddest event that I've ever seen. And in your eyes there's still a glint that looks like mirrors reflecting the sun. Now there's a glowing ring still around you that almost blinds us. A spiritual awakening is what I think you've had, Cy. I've read and heard about how they affect everyone who contacts that person, all in a good way, of course. Your experience can benefit us as well as others."

"You know, Jan, it's as if the whole earth spun around in front of me. I saw people from all lands wave, smile, hug each other. Being fed and filled by great tables with the finest foods were the poor. And there were wines and juices with fruit trees of every variety. Grapevines surrounded it all. People by the thousands were seated, and no one was without a friend. Gone were all weapons of war, and where they were, gardens stood."

"Cy, we may talk more about this later. Mark and Will are fascinated by these kinds of events. What's amazing is that it's real and not only your imagination. After that I hope you can get rest. No one whom I know has ever gone through it."

"Actually, more than in years, I feel at ease, and it's relaxing me to do the job tomorrow. Create a better place to live is what I'm doing rather than only build something that earns me a bit. Have a great night, Jan and see you at breakfast." He sauntered to his room.

"Okay Gramps. You've made it easier for me to rest well. Waiting for you will be the English muffins and your favorite coffee from the Caffeine Cafe."

Few people have the kind of spiritual awakening that Cy had. Many said they have, but seldom can they prove it. Rare it is, but when it does happen, fascinating things can occur in the person's life. Feeling as if they are protected from serious harm, thinking more clearly and doing things better than they have done them before are some.

In other countries, people have even reported them.

Some television ministers may make it look as if people have them, but it's often only a way to bring more people to their services. Some also have had deja` vu, feeling as if they have had an exact experience before and that they are reliving it. Of course, extrasensory perception, where he or she feels something is going to happen before it does has also been claimed. These are events that no one knows about, and only He could fully explain. Being mysteries, some people say they are proved and some not. It's real if we have it.

CHAPTER 12

"Will, time to take a break," Jan said. "If you listen to the songs when you rest, it's all right and may help you remember them. Pet Coon a little so that he'll take his nap, though. Quell those dreams that make him shake sometimes—he's used to Gramps doing that."

"Sure, Mom." So he scratched old Coon's ears and tummy. Laying his head down, Coon flipped his eyes closed. "Good guy. Now you count those squirrels as you nod off. 'Oh say can you see,'" Will chortled as he dozed.

In the future, Will would struggle with his identity as most adolescents do. The desire to snatch fame from the jaws of defeat might confuse him or drive him to attain his goal so early in life that he'd burn out and become a teenager lacking fame, fortune or purpose in life. It befell many before, but he was certain that as the sun rose each day, his mind geared into hyper and pierced the veil of mystery that separates the successful from those who fail. Once he rose, his being could claim a small piece of the world.

Morning broke, and Coon scratched at the door, ready to be let out in the yard. "Arr," he moaned, eyeing Will with a pleading glance.

"I know, time to go," Will mumbled. Ambling to the back door, he let Coon out. "As long as you're here, we get up when we're supposed to," he sighed. "Hey, Mom," he said, glancing in the kitchen where she was cooking an omelet. "Good thing I let Coon out before he sneaked that way." His eyes were bleary and his head fogged.

"Morning, son. Ready for that rehearsal today? I know that you've worked hard for it," she responded.

"Oh yeah, I will be. While I'm waiting for breakfast, and before I go to school, I'll go over my songs." He actually was repeating them in his mind, as he did during any activity.

"Lovely, I'm sure Mrs. Smith will appreciate your endeavors. In school, some fail to go the extra mile. But it's crucial and will prompt success and achievement with anything when you get older. You'll go further in life like that."

"And I'm enlightened by it now. Keep busy and stay happy. If I perform well enough, I'll tutor others, too." He envisioned himself a solo virtuoso giving his heart to all.

"That's the way. You're marching the high road. Following Gramps has been good for all of us, but especially you." She saw Cy's intensity in his purpose.

"Sally Lu and Shannon have been Gramp's other favorite grandkids since he first met them." To them he was never any old guy but the model for a good life.

"As far as I know, even when Gramps was a young man, if he whipped someone in a fight, the next day the loser would be on his porch giving him a bear hug. Then he'd invite Gramps to dinner. There were never any hard feelings for long."

"Morning, Jan dear," Cy said, lodging against the kitchen door sill. "Sweet of you both making me feel so good first thing in the day. Wasn't eavesdropping, but the comments kind of drifted back to me. Coon's lapping tongue had already popped my eyes open, of course." Tears welled in his eyes and coursed down his cheeks onto his pajama collar.

"Well, Gramps, we love discussing that great time in the past when it was easier for us to really care about each other. Through good and bad times a friend stayed a friend. If you both had a problem, each would try to work the other through it. Now until our own is solved, there is nothing left for others."

Friends are friends, and we hope that they will be for years. But now, people move so much, it's a challenge for kids to keep friends. Dad takes a new job out of state, and there goes the friend. Will, Sally and Shannon have been friends a while. They played together and suffered loss together. Friends often share feelings. But through the tough times they support each other. Rich people, poor people, and any working person and persons in school need friends. No matter what we become, famous or not, to enjoy life, it helps to have someone special there. Alone can be a bore after a while.

"At school, too, it's like that," Will said. "Once in a while even the teacher ignores us. They're musing and ask you to return later. I know they're working on their tasks, but it delays our asking for help." He saw several students turn about with their heads hung.

Mark had the kitchen anxious to add his share. "For most of these problems the answer is for the world to work together rather than trying to be lone wolves and tough it out. Sooner or later we'll all depend upon someone, friend, neighbor, family or God. No one is an island, even if they float for years, making it good," Mark added.

"When the ones who made you what you are whittle away from age, moving or going solo themselves, you miss 'em, and your heart will tell you who's king anymore. Surprise, it's not you. Then you start fresh and hope it'll be as good as it was before," Cy admitted.

"When you lose yourself in the shuffle of the world, that's the worst pain of all. Few get to do the work they would love to do and are stuck wailing away at tasks fit for serfs and vassals in medieval days. Any achievement becomes only fabric for mere survival," Mark added. "If we could enjoy what we do, no matter the task, happiness could be commonplace. But that's unlikely to happen."

CHAPTER 13

"That's the best part of building something," Cy said. "Shoving it together causes flaws. Patience is first, and the best follows. If a new house has kinks, the owner expects repairs, but a good worker seldom deals with that."

"Do it right each time," Will said. "Only once is time given, and it has a limit."

"Wasting it is wrong since we can't make more of it," Jan said. "Like Gramps outlasted most of his friends, but years ago he didn't know that would happen. It only worked that way."

"To be sure that time is seen as long, not short, I look to the future and ignore anyone who tells me otherwise. Being around kids who entertain keeps us more joyful. That's the greatest gift to the world. Over the years, Will has really proved that to me. And he's still adding to the lives of you and Mark as well," Cy said.

"In the hands of children is the future, so how they

prepare for theirs is what our lives may become later." Jan credited her parents and grandparents with her accomplishments.

"If our whole country is going to make it, we must tie the knot between children, parents and grandparents. Our family is doing it, but some older people are forgotten by teenagers unless they need them in some way, such as for rides," Mark added.

"In much of the past the home was a scene of cheer, so that young ones would compete to see whose house to take a friend to, where to do homework and probably where to raise their own kids," Cy admitted.

"To live better, a good family eats dinner together and chats about ideas to strengthen them," Will observed. "Years ago we made time to do that, but now many of us eat solo. At least, in many families it's like that."

"Actually, eating alone is less healthy, and we're far better off in groups. That encourages people to care for each other," said Cy.

Eating is part of the heart, not only a social affair. That's why people who eat with others are healthier. The friends and family we are with make the difference. Few people actually enjoy eating alone, although they do it. It's a matter of our life's routine, and the routine is made special when there are others to share it with. Cy and his family knew that, so they chose to eat together. In a busy day it may be difficult to get together. Meal times are, therefore, important times to enjoy.

"Okay, with that said, breakfast is served," interrupted Jan. "Everyone eat well, and give to someone else during the day, since that's the best way. If it were put into practice everywhere, that motto would benefit the world. To volunteer a half hour of time daily to assist anyone is simple." A soul directs one to give freely to others.

"Great point, since we elevate ourselves by helping others. In the best way it usually returns to us," said Mark. "As often as a boomerang returns to the thrower."

"Good comparison. Maybe it won't return directly, but in time what we put out often seems to arrive when we need it most," Cy said.

"But we shouldn't do good expecting to get it back, right Gramps?" said Will.

"You believe it. To smile when doing good, give when others can't return the favor. Some may return it, but by some other means fortune is more likely to come. When you need something, out of air, it's there."

"Like when we do a little extra work on a house at no charge to surprise the owner. Then in the mail we receive a check for a good part of what the cost would have been or more." Mark beamed.

"Or we get a job somewhere that pays for our gas, food as well as a place to stay and are paid far more than we asked for as well," Cy added.

"Yes, you'll seldom get back less than you give when you do for others out of the goodness of your heart," Jan said.

"No matter how it's done, you have to get out of yourself at every possible opportunity. There's work, then play, to serve others. If you make serving part of everyday life, it will be done," said Cy.

"That's why when I study, I explain how to work a problem in math or science to fellow students. Relying on themselves they are more confident to then assist others," Will added. The person he assisted may not always succeed later, but for then it is one more battle won. No one knows the outcome from assisting others, but it's more likely to be positive.

CHAPTER 14

… "Speaking of helping, how about we head for that house and let Will get to that rehearsal today," Mark said. Shaking his hips, he imitated the hula dance, beaming.

"And when this mess is cleaned up, I'll feed Coon, let him out, then head to work. We've got a big counseling load of single moms, a great program to get them to work and childcare for them. Many are entering college and moving up." Jan smiled.

"Great, hon. They really have a weight to bear, and it's often not their fault that they're going it alone. To raise a child, it may not occur to a young guy, can be difficult. As soon as they see what it is, they may leave," Mark said, raising his eyebrows.

"The women mustn't blame themselves. For their families to work for them rather than against them, that's the ultimate goal. Then is when everyone begins to win," Jan responded, twitching her ears and twisting her hair in a knot.

"Well, hope they'll make a new life due to you, Jan. There's a far better chance of it when they have guidance than making choices alone," Mark said. "Take care, and let me know how it's going often. I believe in you, too." He patted her on the back.

Improving others' lives is sometimes the hardest work to do, Jan found. To begin with, many repeat some mistakes that got them in trouble. Or she changes so Jan knows she's succeeding. If they had problems at home, that could log-jam her goals. Her mom and dad may have divorced or argued so the child wanted to escape. Then the young girl may run off with a boyfriend or, worse, alone. Dangers lurked then, Jan knew. She settled conflicts between parents, counseled them with the child but still sometimes failed. If parents assisted, it often succeeded. If Jan could teach others through them observing her family, miracles could happen. Who's given and received a hug today?

"I'll sure let you know. And enjoy that crafting at Dr. McKenzie's place," Jan grinned. She occasionally mused about tossing a tool pack over her own shoulder and beginning her own construction firm after learning the trades. She'd call it 'The Hard Hat Lady.'

Mark and Cy shuffled to the truck, tossing tools and securing the extension ladder. Fixed at the living room window, Coon eyed them, looking winsome as always when his dad left him. Cy flicked a wave that eased him, so that his next object of interest was his food dish. After several bites, he lapped water then hopped up on Will's bed and napped.

"Will, bus coming in five minutes," Jan screamed to remind him to rush getting his books together.

"Okay, I'm heading out," Will blared as he stumbled for

the door. "See you at four, Mom." He yanked his backpack on that read, "Will McGinn, the voice of 2010."

"Today I may be a bit late," Jan said. "You have Dad's cell phone number if there's a problem. Make sure he or Gramps is here if you go out to play."

"Right, got it," said Will and dashed to the curb as the bus screeched to a halt.

"Coon, you behave now," Jan said, pulling a stack of copies from the printer and stashing them in her briefcase. "Don't be looking for ladies over the computer, either," she cracked. Hunting for him is what they'd do. 'Wanted by fancy poodle, hound dog' popped up on the screen when Jan whirled her head away. She'll want a feast, Coon.

"Arr," was all Coon managed as he lay his head back down again.

Jan stepped out, locked up and grinned as she considered how well the world worked if it went according to plan.

Only part of the time was Will a latchkey kid. Often there was someone at home when he arrived. At least Coon would be, and he guarded Will if he was alone. Will called Sally Lu or Shannon for a chat, and they could call. He visited them if he were anxious. One of each of their parents worked at home, so was always there.

Will and his friends labored on homework and played kickball, tag or Wiffle ball in their massive back yards with trees, flowers and a rabbit or two that scurried by. It was always competitive, with no boredom, although they were aware of the occasional stranger who happened by. In the past Greentown had a few crimes, but everyone there was aware of suspicious people. So most problems that plagued other cities and towns in Georgia they avoided. By having strong faith, they managed to stay safe.

Almost safe. As Will dashed for the bus, a silver van squealed by the yard, and an arm snaked out of the passenger window with what he knew was—a gun. He hit the dirt and thirty rounds struck or ricocheted around him, outlining his body perfectly. Then the van skirted the bus and screeched out of sight. Will got up, dusted himself off and hopped to the bus while rotating his head to check for more action. As he entered the bus, the stoic driver gave him a curt glance but avoided the inquiry about what he saw. Will remained mum, shuffled to plop in the back and stuck his head in his history book all the way to school. He decided not to mention the incident to anyone for fear of reprisal.

The three men involved in the incident were of diverse backgrounds, with different agendas for themselves. Most anyone knows that with an excellent ruse, it can be easier to reach goals. Some ethical, some skirting the edge of legality and high in risk.

CHAPTER 15

After buying a few supplies they were short on, Mark and Cy drove to the doctor's estate. When they sauntered to the door, they saw it was ajar when they expected it locked. Greasy spots marred the rosewood floor, and it was redolent with pine.

Half the mahogany wood was missing, and it was obvious that a visitor had helped himself to the quality material. On the ground were scattered a few hundred-dollar bills they failed to see. Blowing in, a strong gust of wind whisked them to the street.

"Better let Doc know that we'll be late going today," said Cy. "He's so time-conscious, you know." He eyed his watch to see they had five hours until dark.

"Sure, it'll take a few hours to round up some of these goods," Mark agreed. He dialed the number. "Dr. McKenzie, please," he stated to the receptionist. The doctor answered in a moment. "Sir, this is Mark. Look's like we've had stolen critical supplies to begin, but we'll be on track shortly." The doctor allowed for errors and told him, fine; have the lumber company bill him directly for the replacements. "Thanks much, Doctor. Over the next few days we'll put in overtime to assure we're on target." The doctor agreed and hung up. As the sun popped in and out of the clouds, a light rain fell.

"Come on, Dad. Let's gather the lumber rather than start out short," Mark suggested. He motioned for them to get in the truck.

"Can you leave me here this time?" Cy asked. "That snake wood takes a lot of patience to work, as you experienced, and at least that can be underway once you get back." His eyelids flickered when the drops grew larger. "Rain, got to get inside," he groaned as he shuffled to the door. Once he entered, Mark called to him.

"No problem," Mark agreed. "That should even us out, and we won't have as much over hours now. Thanks, Dad."

"Try to be back shortly after noon," Cy commanded. "You know how I can be if I miss my fruit and coffee. That new waitress at the Caffeine Cafe is a real gag. She'll make our day." He was a regular there and had his own seat at the counter with his name on it.

"Should be back sooner. I've memorized the list and can finish it pronto. But don't complete before I return," Mark joked.

As Cy set about working the snake wood for the railing, he heard a vehicle out the front door backing into the drive. Opening the door, he saw a stainless steel and chrome panel truck. The back door opened, and all the missing lumber tumbled out onto the ground. Before Cy could see the driver, the truck screeched out and down the road. Ivanik Janawitzke had done his job, but his cohort Angus Johannsen was rarely satisfied.

"Imagine that," Cy said, shaking his head and eying the pile of wood. "He took it and then changed his mind, I guess. It's rare that a thief returns the property."

Eyeing something else, he approached the pile. A three-foot black silk sack tied with a golden chain was underneath. When he removed a few pieces of lumber from the top, he noticed the sack had toppled onto its side and a green color. Through a small split in it, a stack of one-hundred dollar bills had squeezed out. Curious, he shoved the sack more, and a second stack of bills eased out. "Whoa!" he exclaimed. "Someone just plopped a load of loot at our door—uh, the door of the doctor's house." He paced around the sack and eyed the heavens for an answer.

His mind racing and his heart strumming a rapid pace, he considered the source of the cash. Drug sales, robbery, counterfeit. How much was it? A hundred thousand, million, ten million or more? At the least, more than he'd ever see in his life. Now, what would he do? Soon Mark would return, and explaining this one required a steady nerve. Then they'd discuss who to call and how Doc McKenzie or the police would react.

"Now that bag I can't touch, and I'll leave the wood, too," he said. "This is way too much to take lightly." From the stress he sweated and sat on the front step of the porch, waiting for Mark and debating what to tell him. "He'll never believe how this happened," Cy muttered. "And if he does, what's he going to do that I can't think of? If the newspaper gets hold of this, we'll have fifteen minutes of fame but not the way we want it. Greentown won't know what hit them and will wonder where their peace went. Unless Doc McKenzie rides the storm out for us. Of course, he might be connected with the money, so that's a thought." Pondering it, he trembled and gagged.

"Dad, what's with you?" Mark asked, as Cy had failed to see him pull in behind the massive lumber pile. "Only two hours passed, and you look burned out. Hope that wood didn't roll into your head. Hey, looks like someone made a Goodwill clothes bag donation. And that's the material we were missing. You didn't hide it as a bad joke, did you?"

"Be great if that were all true, but things aren't so simple now," Cy said. "First thing is, with the wood returned is a pile of cash. And we have no idea who dropped it, except it was a chrome panel truck. Blacked out was the license plate, and the windows were smoked so the driver was anonymous. Before I could get near it to see the driver, the muscle car engine rushed it down the road." He fidgeted, twiddling his thumbs.

"You can't be saying that some crazy pulled a bank job and simply picked here to get rid of the money. Unless Doc was part of this, and he wanted us here to confuse the people tracking the money sack," Mark added. "Until we're done with it the house is not his, so no one can connect it with his real home."

"The wood was used to veil the cash until he could get here to pick it up, and it still looks like only a building site," said Cy. "If we call to report the money, we'll be the ones questioned first, and anyone else can deny anything about it." His nose twitched and eyebrows flickered.

"Or to finish the job we can use the replacement wood and leave the cash where it's at, like nothing ever happened," Mark said. "That's what we do, Dad, and act as if we're only doing our own work."

"Let's strictly avoid the problem, and it's gone," Cy agreed.

"Sounds good. Once those step plates are done, I've got the varnish, but you work that railing, and when ten steps are finished we'll be able to tack the railing to the wall. Give me that nail gun, Dad, please," said Mark, as he slipped down a few steps and sighed.

So Cy handed him the tool and began his own work while in the driveway about a million or more dollars lay. Dreaming of how easy life could be if they only buried the money for a few years, then took chunks of it outside the country to bank it, they plodded to the window and peered at the rain. But they didn't have the will to follow the urge.

"Dad," Mark asked, "for a couple of woodmen in a state that's low profile, how did something like this happen to us?" He popped five nails into the stair without thinking.

Mark and Cy were at odds on what to do with the money sack. When they thought on it, they sweated and dreamed about the good life if only it was theirs. Before this neither of them had anything like it occur before, and they knew it was like a fantasy that they couldn't be living through. The preacher, Jan or Will could have some ideas how to handle it, but it would be they who got the blame for it if they took it or did too much to cover it up. In their savings accounts were a few hundred thousand dollars, but it had taken years to reach those goals. The sack held a lifetime of savings. If they only knew where it came from, things would be so much easier. Would they ever know the truth?

"That's the idea," Cy suggested. "When a place is no big deal, to spice it up, things happen. Makes life worth the living. And when those involved live in smaller communities it's easier to get by with this."

"You don't think that's why Doc McKenzie is moving to this property in the first place, do you?" Mark asked. "Five acres of land separating him from other houses probably makes him feel private enough to handle money deals?" His face screwed up.

"He could have been in on this way before, but it's obvious no one wants watchers near when they're in way too deep," said Cy. "Part of the so-called perfect plan, if it all worked out right." Because he loved his twins, Doc was unlikely to be involved.

"But someone blew it, because we weren't supposed to be here when the cash came." Mark's mind still swirled with the thought providence was involved.

"No, agree with you there. That's not part of the program."

"You think the drivers-by will ignore the bag under the pile when we're gone tonight, though?" asked Mark.

"There's no reason they're likely to notice it. Unless it's the wood that draws them first. Remember the idea of a 'grab bag' where people could buy a bag of odds for a set price? There would be a table full. Most had junk in them, some better items. You simply took your chances when you bought one. Would you have bought one?"

"Maybe not. But it's something about bags that make any of us curious. Boxes or an anonymous container may get us to try and sneak a peak." In the bag could be Pandora's box, with spirits or demons that escape to wreak havoc.

"Yes, silly ideas got our attention throughout time."

"Wonder what Jan will say when we tell her about this. She has strong moral views about what is right," Mark said. He felt to return it and could only keep it if given by law.

"W is going to really say we're off for not handing the money over to him so he can decide how to spend it," Cy joked.

"I wonder what he'd tell Sally or Shannon if he'd been here."

"It'll be interesting to note what he'll say to us even though he wasn't here."

"For now, maybe we should avoid speaking of it around him. It might really confuse him." By the gleam in their eyes, they might spill the tale.

"Yes, he might not gather it all until we can figure it out for ourselves," Cy said.

"Okay, let's finish up here and think about it going home," Mark said.

"Makes sense to me," Cy agreed.

"You check the rail brackets, Dad, while I finish out the step braces."

"Got it. Looking like a smooth spiral but could use a check on the drawings, Mark."

"No problem. Checking it now and looks like we'll be on time for dinner, after all."

"Jan is a real thinker, so let's discuss this with her. Really knows what's going on in the world," Cy said.

"A woman has that intuition, and it's knowing facts, her experience and people skills that give her the edge reading the cards, that is, making decisions."

"Bet they try to keep them off of the gambling tables in Las Vegas so they don't clean the house out. I've heard that some players were so good, card counters, they're called, as a lot of sharp math is involved, that they're not allowed to play."

"Some really know the game, and the business can make less than the player," Mark said.

"They couldn't prod me into a gaming house. It's not moral and too easy to lose your head." Years ago, he had a friend who won millions but then went loco, risked and lost it all.

"I've heard that many people take only what they can afford to lose in there." He reasoned that this meant it was like a pool that had a limit on what you could bet.

For those who failed to heed the caveat, losses of thousands of dollars for the lure of fast cash had occurred. To avoid it, one should consult family, minister and honest friends. If the money's less available, there's less desire to use it to attempt to beat the odds. Neon and lack of clocks can make too good to be true a bit of treachery. Hand the money to one who holds on to it longest, a safe bet.

"Like that pile of money out in the driveway looks like an easy life, numerous people believe they can make it big in gambling and continue playing, like that battery rabbit," said Cy.

Cy and Mark obsessed about the sack of money but were scared to touch it. There were stories of horrid events that feasted on those who couldn't keep their hands off of what wasn't theirs. Not strictly thieves but ordinary people who had odd things happen and made poor decisions. They had plenty of money in the bank, but it was nothing compared to millions. Maybe it was so easy to come by to test their honesty, and there would really be a reward if they turned it in. But the other side of them said that it was trouble for the asking. They knew that some robbed banks but were almost always caught, except for Frank and Jessie James back in the old West. For the first time in his life, Cy had already been in jail due to a chance event where he was protecting himself.

By keeping funds in the bank, most people protected their money. A cache of money not in a bank made many people queasy. In his overalls and work boots, Cy appeared poorer. He'd still avoid carrying much money in his wallet. He stayed safer, quite an accomplishment.

CHAPTER 16

The stainless steel step van had been driven by Ivanik Janawitzke, a five-foot dynamo with a rock body who was a German nuclear physicist. An epitome of high-tech wares, the van was equipped with a GPS system, military spec radar-jamming unit and a visibility veil to randomly prevent any human eye, as well as police helicopters, from seeing it. The money for it was provided by Angus Johannsen, a Swedish entrepreneur of six-feet, five inches with shoulder-length blonde hair, blue eyes and a chiseled face. He'd made his fortune in minerals and mining futures, lost half a billion in the ravages of Soviet mergers after American-style capitalism began its reign, but he had half a billion left.

"Angus, dropped the cash anonymously. In this area there's an unsophisticated population. No concern about detection," Ivanik bellowed over the signal-identification blockage cell phone. He glared into his pop-up mirror and saw an older man saunter to the sack, then he gloated as he told Angus of his escapade, and in retort Angus snorted.

"Ivanik, you were to drop the cash clandestinely, no people about. If he even glanced at the vehicle, that's risky. You failed to even activate the visibility veil! Remember, your mind is one of the best, but it's my account that's funding this jaunt. If you want those islands, get this right." Angus wagged his head and muttered, "fool."

Ignoring Angus, he smirked and boasted, "It's done. I'm on Central Avenue almost to the interstate. Still picking me up at Hartsfield? Be there in three hours." He snapped the cell phone closed. From the ashtray Ivanik snatched his pipe, depressed some cherry tobacco into the bowl and pursed his lips as he burrowed it in. He flipped a match at it and sucked in with fervor until the plug caught fire. "Ahh, my only vice, except money laundering, that is."

Angus returned over the voice-activated cell phone embedded in the dash. "Sure, and I'll have Bhagran ready to switch doubloons for the cash to confuse them. Leave the truck in the short-term parking lot where he'll find it. And clip that Georgia plate on there now so the cops won't sniff you out. See you in a few." He pocketed his cell phone and scanned for any agents at Trackers, the local lounge for any and all traffickers worldwide coming to the U.S.

"Yo, ready to go." Ivanik veered onto the first exit where there was a truck stop. Behind the last row of rigs he circled and stopped. A few more pipe puffs, and he leaped out. Strutting to the rear of the van, he snapped the plate on. On his mind was his dream, the South Sea coral lagoon that he and Angus flew over a month ago. Coco palms, lush vegetation, banana trees and a few random residents. A real estate check confirmed that it was for sale at ten million dollars, the same amount of laundered money that he donated to some Georgia driveway.

"Hey pardner, you got a lug wrench on that jewel?" a trucker who sauntered to him asked. He was five-feet-five and three hundred pounds with his belly rolling like a giant beach ball over his belt.

Ivanik snapped to attention and groaned, "No sir, only on a spin delivery heading back to the terminal," he lied.

"Okay, have a safe one," and he plodded to the restaurant.

"Time to hit it. This box is drawing the curious." Ivanik sprang back into the truck, started it and hot footed back onto the interstate. For the three hours to the terminal, he scanned radio stations, listened to parts of ten CDs and screened his side view mirrors for the law. With no snafus, he terminated his trip. A few glances from state boys had him wreak sweat, but they gunned their engines to honor his sharp truck, grinned and passed on. Only looking and liking this chrome charmer, he thought.

"Ivanik, you almost here? About ready to huff it to Stockholm. My lady's called five times and threatened to bounce me," Angus snapped over the radio.

"Only half an hour from there. Big birds all over the air. I'm ready to clear out too. Why suffer?"

"Suffer indeed. My half billion loss was no small change. Thanks to capitalism moving into Russia. I bamboozled the KGB, moles, the Kremlin's rulers and Siberia's desolation to become a financial guru. Business and science are divergent. You can blow up Earth, but I can restore it with the right venture. With my new baby electromagnetic pulse generation, I'll collect microbursts of energy from the air to operate any current device that uses any form of fuel." He hesitated.

"Dumping cold cash with no research on where it may

go was idiocy. A financial genius you are, but logic you lack. Let me handle that. We're a team," he growled into the phone.

"Right, nothing like money mixed with alchemy. So far it's worked," Angus said sarcastically.

"Traffic's a pit bull … when I get there." His words broke up. Ivanik had ten minutes to the airport. He mused about boarding the plane and being back in the Marshall Islands, an American protectorate. Upon arrival, he ferreted out a parking space and found it on the top deck. Then he lowered the black side and rear trim to camouflage it. Less visibility, he reasoned, on the top deck. Safer from prying eyes. An observer too close could see the clipped-on tag and lift it in an instant. Once parked, he leaped out and savored the morning sun.

It was fall with a crisp breeze sweeping through his graying shock of hair. Breathing a sigh of relief, he notated his location and strode into the terminal. Angus had his ticket, itinerary and final destination arranged. Through security he passed, only one change of tropical clothes and hat in his duffel, and dashed to the American Airlines gate. From there, he'd connect to a private jet in Honolulu.

Angus called moments before he boarded the plane, which outraged him. "Ivanik, hope you were covert in your transit to the gate. That's why I had you check in at American. Turn now and head to the restroom. I'll meet you there in fifteen minutes. Select a stall and slide your shoes toward the door. I'll note it and enter the one beside it when available. Wait for two taps on the wall, then we both leave five minutes apart. The Lear jet's at the charter terminal, engines whining." He awaited a response.

"I want those islands. Our contract says a hundred million for the job. 'Cause when the prospectors in Brazil see we got their stash, we may be chunked in a hole there." Ivanik reeked sweat and drew glares as he entered the stall and slammed the door. "In here," he grunted to Angus.

"Be there in a few," Angus snapped, eying his plane as he tromped across the tarmac up the stairs to the terminal. In his pocket a World War II .45 bulged. From the threshold he eyed the restroom nearest him, realizing he forgot to ask Ivanik which one he went into. He rang his cell. "Ivanik, Angus here. There are three men's rooms between our plane and the first American gate I see. Give me a number." Upon the wall he noted an ad: "Fly American to paradise." "You have the affliction of running from yourself. I'll keep my word about your dream, but remember mine. Recouping that half billion. I live business; you live escape," he snorted.

"Maybe so, but bombs and power plants aren't me anymore. Off track here. I'm the middle one, first stall to the left," he snapped.

"You're a poor listener. I told you to slide your feet out to let me know your location. You just pigeonholed yourself. Any problem, bet's off. You pay your way back to Hamburg while I go to Stockholm."

"No worry; glanced under the doors and across the stalls. Empty."

"Dead luck. Unheard of in major terminals. Coming." But it was 10 p.m. Angus shuffled to the room and stifled the urge to appear flustered. When he arrived, he washed his hands, brushed his curly mane and eyed the mirror for the right stall reflection.

Sure enough, number one left. Stall number two emptied, and Angus turned to enter.

"Nice to see you, Johannsen. Thought we forgot you?" From behind him, a face Angus etched in his memory confronted him. It was Milos Stalinski, the Polish mole who fomented the major merger which ravaged Angus' major account.

"Thought my assassin killed you. Paid him a million for that hit," Angus huffed.

"He had a problem with his aim. My red dot made its mark, right through the heart." Milos smirked and fished inside his jacket for his .45 with laser sight. The imprint of the barrel against his jacket quelled Angus.

Ivanik stood on the toilet seat, peered over the stall door and thought fast. He snatched a shoe off, took aim and slammed it against Milos' temple.

The eight-foot tall behemoth was about to collapse when Angus realized that they'd all be arrested if he struck the tile. He managed to shove him into an open stall, clambered in behind him and locked the door as Milos slumped onto the toilet seat. Angus kneeled and squinted under the door to check for others, then twirled to Ivanik's direction. Seeing no one at front, he whispered to Ivanik to exit. "Go now to the corporate jetport exit. Head right out the men's room door, go to the stairs, descend and nonchalantly pace to the jet ascent steps. The crew awaits you. In a few moments, I'll trail. He stood rigid until the distinctive clop of Ivanik's polio foot silenced upon his exit.

Ivanik knew there was a risk of being caught. He envisioned half a lifetime behind bars but shrugged the thought away. "Pearls, palms, pristine beaches, perhaps a maiden to marry. Adios to stress. My world," he mused. Once at the portal door, he hopped the steps, and swallowed a grin. As he pounded the outer door open, he eyed the white bird that lead to his pot of gold at the rainbow's end.

A burly crew member appeared at the plane's door. He barked, "Hoof it, man. We've eight minutes to take off.

Word is agents are on the way." The scowl and scarlet face of the sentinel forced rapid obedience.

Ivanik bound the steps with a fervor as Angus marched twenty feet behind. Angus glanced back. Ah, clear so far, he thought. Bhagran has the detestable task. Left behind, poor fellow. Such a dolt he always was.

The pilot shadowed the door. "You've a minute prior to takeoff and a half minute before the door seals." He glared at Angus, clutched the door handle and swept it toward him. Angus squeezed into the one-foot crevice as the pilot stooped into his seat. The engines whined to life as the copilot depressed the switches.

"Have a seat Angus. We've got Bhagran as our marionette. Once he uploads the photos from his cell phone to our files, he gets his share. A million for his job's a windfall. At least he'll get his retreat away from Georgia. His friend in Hawaii's selling a spare house of his for a farthing." Ivanik guffawed, then spat.

"Seen every body of water in the world. Love them, but land and family rule. Enjoy your chunk of rock out there, though. Ring me before you drown or a shark shreds you," Angus cracked with a smirk. Then a rumble rose from his cavernous mouth, as he was humored by his own gaffe.

"If I make it and find the island's not mine … "

"Here's the deed. Certified by the U.S. government, the former owner and the real estate firm." Angus slipped it into his hands as Ivanik's flushed face mirrored his angst and disgust. But he was out of his contract with Angus and free. To be sure, he unfurled the scroll to examine the seals. In his pocket he rummaged for the critical tool, a five-hundred power lumiscope that could detail a micro speck on a blank sheet of paper so that its clarity evidenced any anomaly in its shade, shape, texture and density.

With a trembling hand, Ivanik scoured the document. "Looks authentic. Need a waterproof pouch to protect it." Glancing about, he noted a first aid pack with a double waterlock on it laying upon a shelf. He opened it, flipped the contents back onto the shelf, zipped the deed in the pack and slipped it into his cargo shorts.

Five hours passed in silence before they landed at Los Angeles International Airport to fuel up. At the corporate terminal, a black limo waited on the tarmac, blocking the plane's approach to the gate area. "Out of here; Feds are about to swarm us," Angus bellowed to the cockpit.

"Roger, sir," the pilot acceded. He requested tower clearance, and fortunately the agents had failed to restrict their reroute takeoff. The Lear veered sharply away from the terminal and back toward the runway, taxied and swooshed into flight toward Mexico City.

"We're almost empty," Angus huffed. "But when I had this baby built I knew I'd need a reserve one day. Barely enough to get to Mexico. Mi amigos there know my reputation. Slap a few thousand in their hands for a bribe, and we've a full tank. Then to Honolulu." He fumed at the thought of the botched itinerary.

"Haven't been to Mexico in years. Lucky the stay is brief; pollution drops the birds right out of the sky," Ivanik observed. In four hours they landed at Mexico City International Airport. The contact, Menandano, plunged the pump nozzle into the fuel port while the four occupants of the jet bound the stairs onto the runway for a stretch and a glance at the horde of passengers clambering down stairs of the puddle-jumper twin-engine turboprops.

"Finish, Senor Johannsen. Now for dinero." A smirk crept over Menendano's face as his handlebar mustache flipped upward in response, while his outstretched arm revealed a hook at the end. It was the result of a machete conflict with a fellow bandito.

Angus, in a gesture from his heart, gave the Mexican half a million pesos. "Get yourself a bionic hand. Here's the doctor who'll fit you for it," he sighed. In between Menandano's clamp he placed the money in a black sack and a business card. "Adios, amigo." The four men climbed the stairs into the jet, the pilot slammed the door shut, there was a rapid preflight check, tower clearance, then back down the runway into the air.

"Angus, one more request. I'd like a mil to have a decent living standard there. Snatching fruits from trees gets old soon, and I prefer to eat a bit better. That much is like a buck to you with half a billion still." Ivanik fumbled in his pocket for something.

"I'll lend this to you, but if you don't develop to bring in that much profit in a year, I'll come looking for you." His face creased into a scowl as he shoved another sack of thousand dollar bills at him, so Ivanik knew he meant it.

"Angus, your haughty heart is your tragedy." Ivanik whipped a .22 pistol out and riddled Angus with the six bullets in its chamber. The silencer assured the pilot and copilot could be bamboozled. He laid Angus sideways into the seat with a blanket over him and sat beside him.

For five hours he napped, then awoke to the sight of Oahu out the window. Ivanik flipped the blanket off and noted the wounds barely bleeding. "Lucky me, unlucky you, compadre. Thanks for the Stockholm trust fund," he whispered as he clasped the body with one hand and worked his wallet out with the other. "Won't be needing this." Ivanik dug the double-sealed plastic pouch with the deed out of his duffel bag, unzipped it and tossed the wallet into it, then dropped it back into the duffel and zipped it. He found a parasail, slipped it onto his back and the duffel over his shoulder, opened the cabin door and leaped. "Sayonara. Thanks for the lift, gents," he sneered as he plunged. One of the engines came inches from sucking him into the turbine. He huffed a sigh of relief, pulled the rip cord and glided in circles toward Diamond Head.

Upon landing, Ivanik noted a few tourists visiting the cemetery at Punch Bowl and some big kanakas with their wahines lounging about the edges of the caldera. They ignored him after some sharp glances. As he folded his parasail, he knew that his only route to the Marshalls must be rapid, before the FBI could investigate Angus' murder. Counting Angus' wallet, he found only $10,000 but every brand of platinum credit card.

He climbed to Punch Bowl's top and, once there, had a vantage point how to get to the airport. Hunting the path to ground level, he fumbled through the credit cards and wallet IDs. In the Marshalls, he'd find a local to bribe so he could cash in the cards for a maximum advance. Ivanik had graphics training. Reproducing Angus' signature was a minor matter, and once the wallet was tossed back into the sealed sack, he trudged to the road and found a bus stop. Within ten minutes he was on board one and headed for Honolulu International Airport.

Once he arrived, he checked his person for prohibited items. "The gun," he murmured to himself, "got to wipe the prints, swab the barrel and dump it. Ah, the ocean. Getting late. Got to get a cab this time." Reeking sweat that puddled on the pavement, he found one and sighed to the driver that he wanted a final view in a calmer, more isolated beach area.

"I get you to in fifteen minutes," the cabbie chortled. Rate's twenty dollars. Need a ride back?" The driver craned his neck to grin at Ivanik. He had reached a stand of palm trees fronting the water.

"Give me about ten minutes alone. Need quiet; stressed." Ivanik flushed.

The driver flashed a toothy grin in the rearview mirror. Know your kine problem. "That's why I smoke a little pakalolo each day. No stress then. Smooth sail."

Ivanik hopped out and saw no one. He repeated, "Ten minutes," flipped the driver twenty plus ten for a tip to return then waved him on. Once the cab was out of sight, he waded a hundred feet into the surf, glanced again for watchers, saw none, snatched the pistol from his vest and tossed it fifty yards out. As it plunked into the salt, he whispered, "bye baby; glad I knew you." In minutes, he waded back to shore and yanked his shoes off. "Tracks can be traced," he mused. Shuffling to the road, he skimmed his feet to prevent reading his bare foot prints as well. "Did I read enough crime novels or what?" He smirked as the cabbie drove up.

When the cab stopped, Ivanik plopped in and boomed, "Thanks, brah, gonna miss this, but have an itinerary to keep." Out the window while the driver shuttled back to the airport, he eyed the palms sweep by and swallowed a grin. In fifteen minutes they were back at the airport where he exited, flipped the driver a twenty and five and said, "Good luck; thanks for the memory." Again he patted himself, but this time he knew that he was clean. Jogging to ticketing, he got a one-way ticket to Guam from the Air Pacific counter, passed through security and strode to the gate.

In a half hour the flight would leave, so he slipped his sunglasses on, bought a milkshake and newspaper, then buried his head behind it until boarding was called.

He was last in line and took his assigned seat in the rear. Fortunately, no seat mate there.

Ten minutes later the jet rose from the runway to Guam. "About twelve more hours to my paradise," he muttered to himself. He'd have a long layover before his final flight.

In his mind, visions of his thatched-roof house swirled. Finally he heard the pilot say, "Flight attendants, prepare for landing. Thanks for flying Air Pacific with us, and enjoy your visit to the island." After circling for ten minutes, the plane settled into its approach and touched down a bit rough but safely.

Ivanik waited for all fifty passengers to clear the plane, then marched the aisle to the door and to the stairs leading to the ground. He descended, entered the terminal and dialed his cell. Calling the realtor, Kalaneolo, he explained his deed. It was for life.

The former Hawaiian hesitated, "It's only a few miles to that islet. Not too large. About three square miles. But it has an operating small hotel, some good shops, small cycles and bikes for transport and two vegetarian restaurants. Communications are satellite. Electricity is wind powered. Most foods are locally grown. Transport to mainlands is by Lear jet but only once a month to Hawaii," Kalaneolo rattled on.

"Upon my venture about, I'll find the truth. What you experience is the only truth. We'll be in touch, Kalaneolo." Ivanik snapped the phone closed and pocketed it. For forty-five minutes he meandered in and out of the terminal, bought a latte then gazed beyond the perimeter at the crashing whitecaps. Lovely, he thought, but not quite home. The call for boarding came, and Ivanik again had a rear solo seat. He slid into it, eyed the rapid taxi and take off, then found himself to be landing and entering the Marshalls terminal in what seemed to be mere moments.

Once Ivanik departed the terminal, he explored. From a vendor out front, under swaying palms, he signed out a mountain bike. After a check of the mechanisms, he bound on and shuttled the roads, noting a few lagoons where tropical fish wavered. His hotel finally sprang into view where he skidded off onto sugar grain sand to eye his property.

Into and out of the entrance paraded a host of nationalities, which seemed to secure his income for a while. He cocked his head toward the front desk and the clerk from Oceania, who beamed at each guest and issued a handshake of greeting. Plodding to the foyer, Ivanik strutted to the clerk and whispered to him who he was.

The clerk fidgeted, then offered his hand. "Welcome, sir. Been expecting you." He gripped Ivanik's hand, pumping it, and led him to the owner's office. Ivanik wriggled into the high-backed leather chair, swiveled toward the window that faced the shore and marveled at all that was now his. Through his deception and actions, he'd pursue life with a passion until it all disintegrated.

CHAPTER 17

Continuing his philosophy, Mark said, "We've done it the right way, Dad, saved our pay, invested carefully and worked hard and steady over the years. Used our heads and didn't live at the stores," said Mark.

"Our families get our time like they are supposed to, and the rest of life takes care of itself," Cy said.

Tithing is a difficult habit to develop, but tales of the wonderful experiences of those who tithe are known. Exceptionally positive events that appeared to occur due to seeing the Book as a guide to help get us ahead, not hinder us. Keeping the faith, living to a sound belief and sensing what is right without constant prodding may be the best for most who wish to remain healthy. No need to become a monk, but being with others of like faith and belief is the way to trust yourself. When you move forward, glance back only to remind you where you must trod on to. Love, life, family, friends and job that value your faith are goals.

"When you spend a lot of free time together, doing your own thing seems like the odd man out routine," Mark said.

"We need to be solo at times to recharge the mind, but those with no friends or family can have it rough," said Cy. He thought of orphans who might feel they are alone with hundreds surrounding them.

"Or if you know so few people that you lose some due to age or relocation, that can make life more difficult, kind of like the man who only has his wife as a friend. They grow old together, and if she passes first, he can be the lonely one with no clue how to be happy again. Avoid it by reaching out to God for purpose, accomplishment and goals."

"Yes sir, friends are better in numbers," Cy agreed. "But they need to be real ones, as there are plenty of sunny Sams who won't tough it out when their life has bumps or ruts."

"Maybe we should test them by creating bumps for our buddies to see which ones will make it as true friends. It would sure be a hazard to think that they'd be gone when the real rock was in the road."

"Again, it all begins in the family who teaches us how to relate to our own kin but is also critical for us to succeed on the job, with friends and in being happy with ourselves."

"Being alone with yourself is far better than feeling lonely with yourself," Mark said. "And the strength to spend time alone is in the blood. Some of it can be learned, but the spirit of holding on is really from how we grew up. There are lone wolves, pack wolves and lone-pack wolves."

"So the lone-pack wolf is the best kind of person to be since you can do as well on your own as around others. You feel good no matter how you find your house," added Cy.

Friends can be there for you when family isn't. They can come up with ideas that you can work on together. Play games, travel, spend time talking, and know that they can have a place in your heart, too. If you take and don't give, that can cause friction.

Due to physical or emotional problems, if you are unable to give, friends and family can help you work through some of it. They may be unable to solve all but can remove stress from you when you ask them to be there for you. Trouble is something you don't need. Mark, Cy and Jan are all friends as well as family. Will gives of his time for friends Sally and Shannon and family. The squall Will had with Shannon was soon forgotten, but Sally would dwell over it. Blaming it on Will, she asked that he apologize to Shannon for him to open her heart. Young people can forgive easier than adults, and Sally forgave Will, as we are supposed to do. It meant that Will had to forgive himself, too. During a squall with schoolmates, he knew to open his heart.

"When someone finds a stash of cash like we have and turn from it and to God instead of trying to count it, due to curiosity, that's honor. Excess money, no matter how it happens, may quell many people," Mark said.

"That's why Jan and Will have a say about the money," Cy suggested. "The more minds we put to the task, the more likely the right direction it'll go."

"Will musn't ask Shannon or Sally for their opinions first. This is our family matter, to be settled totally within our family. We need to click together."

"Oh mercy, no. They're really bright and honest, but it's accidental words to their parents that may uncoil the snake and wreak havoc for us. We'll deal with it on a small scale now, then be more open later. Besides, young people get really confused when you speak of large sums of money that appear from nowhere."

"What do you say we call it a day and lock up so we can start solving this mystery?" Mark glanced at his watch.

"We've done a few more hours' work than we thought, and Doc will be fine with it once he knows it."

"Sure. We'll call him tomorrow with the progress report. And deal with the money then as well," Cy said. They both grabbed their tools, but left the ladder.

Mark and Cy shuffled to the truck, turned to eye the money sack a last time, and both sighed, trusting that they'd know what happened in time. It was also a bit nerve racking considering that the money would still be unsecured overnight. They stepped into the truck, took a seat, belted and backed out, driving home like anyone who'd never seen a fortune that day. It would be a long night, and sleep would be tense. But then some answers may come, they hoped.

They'd never dealt with a problem like this before, and it would require discussion. They would talk to Jan, Pastor Jaba and Will to find their attitudes on all of it. Then through prayer and meditation, the best answer would emerge. After waiting a few days, they'd analyze it to be sure that it all made sense, as it didn't now. But finding a lot of money, especially in the millions, was something that few people had experienced. It was rare and frightened them.

CHAPTER 18

They pulled into Mark's driveway, and Will ran up to the truck, bounding and beaming like the Cheshire Cat. As Will eyed Mark's window, Mark forgot his own dilemma for the time and cracked a smile in return. His son was joyful, so Mark was.

What he had to say must have been a big deal. When Mark got out, he listened.

"Dad and Gramps, Mrs. Smith gave me a leading part in the play. I earned either the leading role or supporting actor. Anyway, from where I was this morning, it's a step up. There were twenty auditioning, too. One day I could open for Clay Aiken."

"Son, I'm impressed and way proud to know you're already on a track to doing well in life. This calls for one of those real bear hugs," Mark said as he curled his long arms around Will, grasping him long enough for a few tears of joy to stream down his face onto the boy's bristling green mane.

Excessively encouraging Will's hopes, Cy let it slip out. "W, are you telling us you're going to be a big shot, as a Billy Joel song says? In a few years, if we want to see you, we have to fly to LA or Hollywood?" Cy cracked with a nervous twitch of his nose, like a rabbit.

"Hold on, I'm working on it. Try not to be one of those hard-hand stage dads. One day we can be well-known, then it's back to the real world, having to peck at our food like a chicken to make it," Will said. In pensive thought, he hung his head momentarily.

When young people were successful in any creative area, especially acting or music, their careers sometimes peaked once they were adults. Then there was a search for themselves beyond the celebrity of youth. It took much readjustment and a return to the real world of the average life with a fraction of the money and the struggles and yearnings of those people. From higher to lower on the ladder of success was often traumatic.

"Didn't mean to seem aggressive, son. Guess we began thinking it's us starting over. To succeed if I had a creative talent, I'd sweat until I might fall apart. It's a dream of many Americans to be respected and followed. Only by living it do you know it, although you can read about the life," Mark said. "I believe that gaining fame even in Hollywood is easier on you than getting on the local news where those who may know you personally can question your integrity. The stress of it can damage even a strong person."

"Most don't want fifteen minutes of fame without respect," Cy said. "Especially fame or a sack of cash that appears from nowhere while you're working."

"Dad, let's see how Jan's doing before we start on that.

Come on in, all of us, and take it easy for a few before we tell the story about the greenbacks of the glory," Mark said.

"I'll go work on tomorrow's songs and really pore over today's, so I'm the best one for the job when cuts are made for the show," Will said. "My first audience is old Coon, and he sure won't throw any fruits if he dislikes it." Will's stomach rumbled, the anxiety of his stage expectations weighing on his mind. Positive thinking didn't eliminate chinks in confidence, even for experienced performers.

Mark chided Will, as he knew that the boy may become obsessed with a dream and fail in the real world. "In all your studies, do well, though. Even for the creative arts, all skills are needed." A firm belief in knowing your odds and risks was mandatory.

"I know, Dad. Because knowledge allows a world of understanding, as you say." He told his dad and Cy that he'd make two calls. Guilt consumed him, he said, and he had to eliminate it.

With his green hair, Will wondered if he could make it in music. Green hair was rare. But even more important was that he had doubts, and you have to know to be a success in a creative field and associate with other creative people. For him, with both school and long practices, it was rough. Although Sally Lu and Shannon were devoted, they had no major part in the play. Why was life that way, he reasoned? There were activities he could do that were not so competitive but not nearly as exhilarating. He called Sally Lu and Shannon to share his feelings.

Will waited for calls from his friends, but they expected his apology first. He called Sally. "Hi, Sally. To begin, I'm sorry about my squall with Shannon," then admitted, "you're as valuable in the play as I am. I was lucky to be awarded a lead part, although I labored. You're one of my two best friends, and I need you." In his eyes tears welled and his mind swirled.

Sally hesitated then groaned, "Will, I forgive you for quarreling with Shannon, but call him. Tell him you care. In this world staying close is the key. To me you'll remain unique; for life we'll be one. Later, as adults, we may separate, but that's temporary. Our hearts and souls will ever bond and know that we're there for each other. That's us."

Will swallowed his pride to grasp the moment. If he failed to reconcile, regret would prevail. "Thanks Sally. You've lifted my spirits. It was apart for a few months. I was so immersed that I forgot what meant most, having my friends, and through time I'll keep you, for good or bad, to complete my life. For me, family is the best, but they can't be there constantly, and you can. As much as possible, we'll connect. See you later and cheers."

"I'll do that, Will, and you do the same. God bless your heart, mind, body and soul," she said and hung up. Smiling, she knew that Will would live for the day, too.

Hesitating to call Shannon, Will remained leery. As he called, Shannon was rehearsing for the play but answered. "Hello, who's calling?" Shannon blurted.

"It's Will; want to make amends." There was a silence. Will's head drooped and he shed tears as he spoke. "Sorry about the fight. Really need you as a friend. Since then, I felt rotten."

"Why should I believe you, Will? You've said that before, but we crossed swords. It's a joke," Shannon growled with a distrusting scowl, tapping his feet.

"Well, I called Sally Lu already and apologized for it. She forgave me right off," he moaned, as his hands quivered with anxiety.

"Okay, let me consider how I feel. Since then, I've lost

sleep but felt better lately. It never happened. In my body and my heart I ached," Shannon sighed. He knew that Will was his best friend, so he'd drop it. "We'll try, but this is it," Shannon warned.

To admit wrong was difficult, but he did. "Sure, been praying lately and asked for strength and wisdom for the future. Next in importance to God are family and friends. It takes time to make them and you can lose them in a flash. So, sorry and will keep peace. We'll begin anew. It'll be you and Sally Lu, because if I succeed, it's due to you and hard work," Will continued.

Shannon felt Will was serious, so he conceded. For years they'd confide in each other in times of need. Shannon told Will bye and hung up, then prayed for guidance. Within his heart a presence swept him out of the doldrums. He envisioned times of hardships his family would experience. His dad and mom debated about teenage travails he anguished over. But always there was God and an earthly friend to light his path. When errors were made he read the Bible, perusing its wisdom. Hours or days later, solutions popped out so he'd heal with his heart strumming.

The conversation at hand reverted to Will being advised to excel in other than music to do well in his life. He harkened to the tune.

"Those in music and drama study many other subjects while acting or singing," Mark said, "to negotiate the winding roads of life." He recalled his hours of research in the library and Bible study that led him out of numerous dark corridors.

"Learn by observing plays, musicians and life," Cy said.

"Thinking is the link to success," said Will.

Will couldn't focus at times. His mind was hobbled by fantasies of the stage, where thousands of watts of hot spotlights seared through his silk Japanese shirt and tai-lored cotton twill, tangerine-colored pants. Fans, especially pretty ladies, squealed his name. He threw bouquets of orchids to them as he rode a carousel, smoke emitting from the horses' nostrils. At his finale, he bowed and leapt into the audience with a flourish, as they begged for an encore.

"Yes, always in life think first to get it right," Mark said, failing to consider consequences of his actions bred emo-tional conflicts. He and Cy had to assure that Will never acted in haste. It was an inherent trait that he seemed not to have but must never have.

"Repeating a song so many times, I contemplated until my head ached. Ginger ale was my best friend and some days, aspirin," Cy added. "But relaxing kept me on track."

"Listening instead of talking can knock out the problem pronto," Mark said.

"We have two ears and one mouth, to listen twice as much as we talk," Will remembered. His third ear was his mind that heard songs in his sleep.

"That's it," Cy said. "Listening more allows us to relate to others for success." An internal voice, likely angels or God, spoke to him and led him ahead. No matter the size of the throng of humanity he encountered in his early years, the voice of guidance continued urging him toward enlightenment.

Music and finding money conflicted. In the McGinn family no secrets were harbored and discussing prob-lems normally solved them. Keeping it in led to rifts of unhappiness.

So in God's hands they placed stress. He was the only one who advised and directed them. They dwelled on the money again, because it must be dealt with to de-stress.

Currently, it was a burden that afflicted them with confusion over values.

"How about asking Jan what she thinks about our situation?" Mark asked. "I mean you and me, Dad." He didn't really trust Jan on this but said it to please Cy.

"Wise suggestion, Mark. Two minds aren't always better than one, but the third mind completes the triangle," Cy said. Geometry entered into some of his conversations.

Ambling in the door, they saw Jan finishing the chicken gumbo, Cy and Mark's favorite dish. The scent wafted to the door, and Coon paced the hall, halting every minute to eye the steaming pot on the stove. His ears wriggled and his nose cocked toward the ceiling, sifting the meat from the spices.

"Coon, wait your turn; you can't eat our food. The vet says no way," Will scolded, glaring at the dog. "Your own chow is the best, and you love it." At that, Coon slinked away to the living room and watched the "Animal Planet" that Jan switched on TV. "Good boy," Will said as he noted his changed interest. He stroked his silky head fur and scratched his chest as the dog flipped over for a belly rub.

CHAPTER 19

"Hey guys," Jan said. "I didn't hear you come in, but Doc called to be sure things went okay and asked how far along you were."

"Doing well, about one-fourth done, and it's as perfect as he'd expect it," Mark said. "When we thought some supplies were missing there was a delay, but they were returned by the scoundrel who took them." He hesitated and glanced at Cy to finish the story. Cy scoffed at him, refusing responsibility for it. After seeing the sack, he thought it would disappear but ... Once they debated it, a direction was decided to resolve it.

"Under the lumber that a stainless-steel step-van dropped before it sped off was a large sack," Cy huffed. "It was full of greens, and they weren't veggies. Money. Cold cash and more than I've seen up close in my life. Like some insane movie or book, and we have no idea where it came from."

"Didn't you report it to anyone or try to call Doctor McKenzie, since it's going to be his house?" Jan asked. "Tell him about it whether it's something he may know or not. If he thinks you don't know, it's out of control." She grimaced and glared at them.

"The idea we had is that we never saw it," Cy responded. "A carpenter and his architect dad build great houses, but taking part in fantasies of finding treasures is the stuff of teenage novels. In real life it may have occurred, but rarely, so you seldom hear of it."

"But it's going to make you wonder what happened for a while, and you don't want it to disturb your life," Jan added, her nerves rattling so she dropped and shattered a plate she'd washed.

"The problems being involved in these situations are far worse than forgetting about it," Cy said. He mused about tossing the sack in a nearby pond that was off the road. But if a fisherman snagged it, another innocent party was in for questioning. Seeing themselves stuck with the dilemma, he'd continue to ponder its finale.

"We'll go back tomorrow, and it was imaginary. The bag is gone, we get to work, and Doc never mentions it," Mark hoped.

"I had a fantasy about burying it somewhere for a few years, waiting for any clamor from it being missing to die down and … " Cy began.

"Then hiding it in a foreign bank so you could blow it as you needed it," Jan finished. "In the Cayman Islands, likely."

"You know how it's done from what you read before, right?" Mark asked.

The conversation was getting tense. After thinking about what they knew, they saw that divine intervention was needed. They clasped hands, began to pray and a flash of light bolted across the room, opening their hearts to their voice of guidance. Much of their concerns drifted away. A breeze swished by, ruffling their hair. Popping in, Will was not about to miss the affair.

"Hey, I'm being ignored," Will snapped. "It's better than anything that I've read in English at school or in the library." His eyes bulged as he hammered his fist on the table.

"Don't dream about living like some king in a big palace," Mark said. "The money's not ours, and we know nothing about it." He sighed and saw bills fleeing from him.

"What are you going to do with it if it's still there tomorrow?" Jan asked.

"We'd have to call Doctor McKenzie anyway. Because of a situation we had nothing to do with, we're not leaving a job," Cy offered.

"We'll take a picture of the open sack. Then, if anyone questions us, it's obvious we saw it but proved we left it like it was and had no interest in it," Mark said.

"If Doc acts innocent, and no one comes to collect the bag, we'll decide what to do then," Cy remarked. "On this one I'll talk to the preacher, as he won't take sides, so we'll know what to do."

"Good plan, Dad. Pastor Jaba will draw on that Chilean culture to make a wise path for us," Mark said.

Pastor Jaba had been all over the world and knew cultures that the McGinns couldn't hope to. He'd probably dealt with the rich and the poor. Whether he was familiar with someone who was suddenly rich due to some odd situation was a challenge. It wasn't like they inherited it. By accident or fortuitously this money appeared. It was not winning a lottery or some contest to get it. Even a pastor needed to dwell on it and figure out who to call, what to ask and what to do with it if the McGinns were allowed to keep it. This would be tedious, so he would ask himself a lot of questions that likely wouldn't come up in his lifetime. But he'd know what do with it if the McGinns got to keep it. This would be work, but he'd be ready.

"What happens if we're given it?" Will asked. "Like going from Mr. Little to Mr. Big."

"The real you or me is not what we have but how we treat others, W," Cy said. "I'll keep working but maybe take a bit more vacation." Vacations were what they missed. For five years it was work with little time off.

Even God rested on the seventh day after creating Earth, universe and man. Home may have been where the heart was, but seeing the country and the world was what they craved. The Andes in Peru, Himalayas of Nepal, kangaroos and koalas of Australia, Taj Mahjal in India, Mount Fuji in Japan and the Black Forest of Germany.

"How about calling Pastor Jaba to see about going by before work?" Jan asked. "By doing that early you'll be fresher."

Mark made excuses and fumbled with his watch. "With his long hours, he needs time to himself. Let's give him a respite. His wife Sheila is out on the street with Bibles, and she's his advisor," Mark grumbled. So he waited half an hour and delayed dinner. When dialing the number he drummed his fingers. Jaba answered. "Hi, Pastor, Cy's son, Mark, here. There was a unique event today to discuss."

"You'll bring your father. He's been quite a mentor to the seniors here," said Jaba.

"Yes," Mark responded. "Dad will come, too. As I am, he's stumped what to do."

"I have critical business to attend to at noon. Please be here by nine," Jaba said.

"Sure, we'll be there by nine." That'll still give us a full day on the job. Thanks. See you then." He grinned and hung up. "He's as sharp as ever to solve this and get us on our way," Mark said.

When Jaba hung up, he pondered the phone call. On mining expeditions in South America, he trekked where millions of dollars in gold was found. In the wilds and courts men, women, families and companies fought over it. People died in conflict. So it was high risk, reason to bow out of the McGinns' affair. But he never denied risk and pressed onward. He wanted to believe in leprechauns. Their gold was in pots, though, not sacks buried beneath lumber piles.

"Well, Dad," Will suggested, "I hope we help people if we finally get the money, but let's treat ourselves some, also." He envisioned Shure microphones with multiplex mixers and Peavey amps.

"Oh, we would," Jan agreed. "But wealth won't control us or change who we are."

"We've always worked for our living," Cy admitted, "and there's no chance of that happening, since we don't go with the flow."

CHAPTER 20

"Great, now that it's settled, the gumbo awaits," Jan said.

Coon had eaten and was in the yard scampering after squirrels, so it would be a peaceful dinner this time. As they were seated, each thought how carefree life is with no monetary concerns. Along with that came travails of the wealthy and their lifestyle.

"This is the best you've made," Mark said. "It surpasses dinner out. Of course, any meal that love goes into is best." In response to an unfamiliar taste, Mark scrunched his face but grinned as Jan glanced. "There's enough spice in here to burn a hole in the sun." His face flushed purple as he gagged and sucked down a pint of water.

"If it's intolerable I'll flush it and slap sandwiches on the table." As she jerked Mark's bowl away, he snatched it back, splattering the gumbo onto the floor. Grabbing a towel, Will knelt to wipe it up, but Jan intervened, flipping her hand to wave him away. "Two hours I labored over that. The spice was added since you complained about it being bland before. Make up your mind what you want," Jan snapped.

Mark stormed from the table, clambering upstairs to pray for fifteen minutes. Once he dropped to his knees and squinted into a trance, visions floated to him of his afterlife. The tunnel of light he saw was dark and seemed endless. Snapping his head up, he saw flickers of lightning dash across the room into swirling balls of flame, then disappear through the roof and walls. As he arose, his feet floated to the stairs where he descended to the kitchen. "After some thought, I see that my tirade was wrong, Jan. Let's get back to peace."

"As long as you eat what we do with no qualm. Coon will slurp it if you won't," she responded.

"Maybe I'll eat his food, and we'll trade tonight," Mark cracked. Jan scowled but remained silent. Cy broke in with a distracting comment.

"If Mark and I went to basic chef classes, one of us would have been at the wheel with you, Jan," Cy apologized. "Trying to help you now without culinary suave might even send Coon packing, ha, ha," he added.

"For sure, few jump in and get it right. Art is putting it all together to please the palate," Mark said.

Spinning her head, Jan saw a masked face with pointed snout and thin paws eye her. It was a raccoon. With teeth bared and tail flicking rapidly, it leapt to the table as the three scattered. Ravenously lapping up all three bowls of gumbo, it then hopped onto a chair. As Jan watched it lick its paws, she wondered where it came from. It must have sneaked in when Coon was let out. Standing on its hind legs, it drove the three backwards.

"Do something, Mark," Jan pleaded. "It may jump on us next. It's staring at Cy, and he'll be hostile if he's bitten."

"Okay, fella. We'll introduce you to our pest extractor." Opening the door, he bellowed at Coon to come in. "Come on, get it out," Mark said. Coon bounded and snapped at the raccoon, saliva oozing from his jowls.

"Arrgh, ark, ark, arrgh," Coon growled. Leaping at him, the raccoon shot over his head. Cy opened the door, but the coon was feisty. It hopped onto the table again, but this time Coon had its number. The dog lunged at it, clamped his teeth into its neck and straggled to the open door, tossing it into the yard, where it loped to the fence and lumbered over it, then dashed off.

"Now that our unwanted visitor is gone, back to our discussion," said Jan.

"Some cook with all their hearts and still get blank faces from their diners," Mark said. "Luckily, only Jan graces us with good food. I think that we'd play chef and fail." His limit was half-cooked eggs and rock cookies the birds wouldn't touch.

The McGinns seldom ate out. Inviting friends and neighbors over occasionally, they made it a real social event, and couldn't enjoy cracking jokes, hugging each other, playing cards, Scrabble or other board games where crowds were elsewhere. At a restaurant Will boomed out some tunes of the Beatles, like "The Long and Winding Road" or "Something," if not more modern hip hop songs or "The Dance" that Garth Brooks sang. Restaurant patrons flipped him onto the table stage to perform. While the manager gawked in awe, he'd croon. If the McGinns dined near home, Coon sniffed them out and wandered into the restaurant. Cy consoled him, put him in the car to wait and tossed him a bone and hamburger to cheer him. Howling to Will's songs, Coon drew cold stares.

"I'm eating lightly," Will said, "since singers have a hot stage with all those lights and audience. The thinner they are, the stronger they perform." He picked and nibbled his food, having little appetite anymore.

"That's right, W," Cy said. "Elvis flooded the stage with sweat, and at the side we kept a pitcher to soothe his throat between sets of three to four songs. Throughout the day before the performance, he'd guzzle water."

"As any other job, music is work," Jan said. "Sticking to it every day, staying in shape and eating healthy are the keys." With fruit bars, juice and spring water, she provided healthy snacks. Except those chocolate mousse mint ice cream cones they ate for treats.

Mark felt guilty for neglecting Jan. "Speaking of that, there are plenty of fruits, the good sweets, on hand. After your hard day, thanks for getting them Jan," Mark said.

"Being exhausted, I needed you. There was one item to get for the gumbo and few shopping today," Jan said. "On weekends you assist, but during the week I need help, too." She tossed the sack onto the table. "Put that away," she demanded. Mark did.

"Each day Dad and I struggle, but I'll scrounge up time to shop for you. It's the task I dislike the most." Mark sighed and glared at the floor. "Dad, how about you help by splitting the time in half?"

"Mark, we'll teach Will some responsibility. He works around the house, but it's time he assists all around. Until he becomes a wealthy song artist, he'll have to help himself. So let's teach him now, okay Jan?" Cy asked. He hoisted his tool pack.

"We'll start him next week. With his rehearsals he's on overtime."

"A week it is. We show him first, then wean him to be on his own." Mark said.

"Think we'll all take a jaunt this weekend," Cy said. It was Thursday. "I've wanted to visit the new section at the wildlife refuge. It draws more birds than before, so I'll try my new binoculars and write in my journal."

"Hey, that book I bought last year will come in handy," Mark said, "with color prints and identifying features of a few hundred birds."

"The refuge has lions, tigers, giraffes, elephants, chee-tahs, antelopes, wildebeests, rhinoceroses and hippopota-muses now," Jan said. "I read about them."

"That means we keep aware," Cy said, "since those large mammals can attack and kill. If that problem at Doc's hasn't been solved, there's time to think about it then."

"Let's go to the refuge today, Dad. I can't wait to see those animals." When an old friend with wealth invited him, Mark had traveled on safari to Tanzania, Kenya and the Congo three years ago. It would be like a return to Africa. There they slept in tents, nudged their rickety Humvees through drilling dust storms and were often stalked by the very creatures they sought to observe. Before going on the escapade, all were briefed of the risks but endeavored ahead anyway. Memories of the thrills were framed in videos that they brought back.

"It's getting late and we have only a few hours, so let's go," Cy said. They bid Jan goodbye, went to the truck and in a half hour drove to the refuge.

As they entered it, they saw groves of pines, scrub, ponds for the hippos and elephants to bathe in and for the animals to drink from, acacia trees for the giraffes to feed upon and grass two feet tall on both sides of the trail as far as the eye could see. Mark stopped the truck for a moment.

Getting out of the truck, Cy saw a tiger and absent-mindedly meandered toward it. It eyed him and stalked as it would any other prey but backed off fifty feet from the truck. So when Cy stumbled, the tiger bounded for him. Mark saw it and tossed a tree branch at it, which only inflamed it.

"Hold on, Dad, I'm coming in the truck." Mark hopped in the seat and slammed the shifter into drive.

"Son, run, it's going to kill me anyway. Save yourself!" were the last words Cy said before the cat was upon him. "I've got to win, God give me the strength," he screamed to the beast. "Got to grab his throat," he said, rolling like a log to avoid its clawed force.

"To distract him, Dad, I'm going to circle you close. Don't roll under me."

"Going to thrash it when I clinch its throat," Cy groaned.

The tiger eyed Mark in the truck nearing it. When Mark was ten feet away from Cy and the tiger, the beast backed off and pounced on the truck.

"Son, slam on the brakes and put it in reverse," Cy screamed.

"Got it, Dad. This should get rid of it." In the meantime, a distant wildebeest drew its attention. The tiger sprang from the truck and gave chase to its prey. The wildebeest dashed away, so the tiger failed to catch it, but it had saved Mark from a tiger battle.

Mark stopped the truck, cut it off and strode out to check on Cy. He was still on his stomach, face down. Mark asked, "You okay Dad?" As he hunched over his dad, who remained motionless, his face was crimson. Mark wept when he saw Cy roll over with a grin on his face. His shirt was shredded, but there wasn't a scratch on him.

Cy offered Mark his outstretched arm and hand. Mark reached out and grasped them to yank him up. Cy curled his arm around Mark's neck as they walked to the truck. "Prayer really worked that time, son. Everything was timed in my favor. See the tiger in that grove of trees looking really confused? Think we'll stay in the truck and on the trail this time. The view's just as good," Cy observed.

Reaching the truck, they plopped on the seat and closed the doors. "Dad, between being brave and being a fool there's a fine line. You were on the line. Let me decide when to leave the truck again," he chastised. "I was the one who traveled on safari. Tigers were the least of our risks. They are Asian, not African. Hippos rushing our boat in the river, elephants on stampede, Gaboon vipers writhing from low tree branches and parasitic worms in the drinking water. Those were lurking, waiting to snare us," he huffed, beads of sweat now popping up on his forehead.

"Thought I was tougher than I was," Cy admitted. "We were unarmed, and the rangers here always carry rifles with scopes. Their vehicles are Humvees. More than a few of them were attacked while in them."

"Dad, look at that giraffe chomping the acacia. With those thorns on the trees, how do the giraffes avoid being stuck or choked?"

"Their mouths are flexible and resist the spikes. Once they've chewed them enough, they swallow them like grass." Cy digressed. "Hippos are more hazardous than crocodiles in the water. They're fast swimmers and territorial. The two-foot teeth and mouths that open almost four feet are their weapons."

Mark drove them next to one of the ponds, and they

eyed the hippos for several minutes. "Watch it, son, here come three of them rumbling for land," Cy warned.

"One of them is the leader. Its mouth is agape and then closes, thrashing the water and forcing the others away. They rush him right after that and threaten to take a chunk out of him," Mark said. They were twenty feet from the pond edge, and Cy sensed danger.

"Take off, Mark. In a moment they'll be upon us."

"Can't start it. What's wrong with this?" he barked as he smashed the accelerator to the floorboard. The first hippo was out of the water and charged them. It was the leader. Several more swam up with the other two.

Slam, roomp, clang, the truck sounded as the over two-thousand pound hippo crashed his jaws against the truck's tailgate. It lurched the truck forward five feet and slammed Mark and Cy's heads against the roof.

Cy hung his head from the window and roared, "horahhh, horahhh" then slammed his right fist against the outside of the door. "Lay on the horn, now Mark, now!"

Mark honked for a solid minute and noticed that the pair of hippos in the pond swam to and fro, then crowded side-to-side before they stilled and eyed the leader. "Hey, the tough one has backed off, flicking his ears and swishing his tail. Now he's plodding around the truck with his head bobbing. He's lying down. Why?" Mark asked Cy.

"It's a sign of submission. The sounds were similar to what a more dominant bull would make. See how the other hippos swam away from shore now. A number are flicking their ears and flashing their teeth to warn other animals away. Try starting the truck again."

Mark turned the key and the motor roared to life. "I'm steering around him, Dad. Stay aware. Okay big boy, see you," Mark said as he veered past the hippo that still lay on its right side, as if tranquilized. Its eyes gazed at the two while its legs wriggled, but it otherwise remained motionless.

"Only one more visit, to the giraffes, son, then we'll go home." They look frightening due to their height, but they don't eat meat. They're vegetarians."

"Dad, haven't you had enough, or are you a glutton for fear? Do you know how to quell their attacks? With their twenty-foot necks, they could topple this truck onto its roof."

"They have much less tendency for violence than our other friends. Their feet are dangerous but can't pierce metal this thick. We'll only be here ten minutes, as the preserve closes in twenty."

"This is the last time I come if anything happens. You come on your own."

"Can't blame you, son. We'll not agitate the giraffes. There's some now, congregating among the trees," Cy noted. "Note that light orange coat with black splotches. Their tongues are over a foot long to reach high branches."

"I'm glad they're tamer and prefer eating so much. Their bodies look too short for their necks. At least if they have teeth, they're too small to damage us," Mark said.

"They usually only lash out at people chasing them on foot and wielding spears, as some tribes in Africa do. Or to animals like lions and cheetahs that would prey on them."

"I remember that, and the safari guides wouldn't allow the rangers to shoot the cats."

"I don't like the thought of big cats jumping giraffes, but the rangers didn't interfere since it's the nature of Africa that some animals prey upon others. The cycle of life," Cy said.

"They're eyeing us, Dad. Those looks, with large round

brown eyes, make them appear to be thinking of their real home. I can see them on the savannah, galloping like wild mustangs on the prairies. Let's get home ourselves. I'll dream of them tonight."

"So will I son. They etch a place in your mind."

Mark wheeled the truck around and drove the trail to the gate, dust swirling in its wake. In silence they drove home, musing about the wonders they'd seen. When they arrived, Cy spoke first. "Mark, let's get back to what was bugging us before, the money sack that stole our sleep." Entering the house, they eyed Jan in the living room.

"How was the visit to the refuge?" she asked, flipping her fingers through her hair.

"Other than a tiger attack on me and a hippopotamus banging the truck, it went fine. Thank the Lord and Mark, we got out of it unscathed," Cy groaned, still perspiring.

"Better wait a while until rangers are on duty to return," she advised.

"Without a doubt, that's exactly what we'll do. I'm no wildlife specialist," Cy agreed.

"Yes, we were blessed to leave there in one piece. Tomorrow we have more challenges. In the morning we'll have a lead, though, with Pastor Jaba. Some people have had real puzzles for him, but it never ceases to amaze me how he has most of them singing praise when they leave his office. He's not your normal advisor," Mark said.

"Maybe he had one of those spiritual experiences I had last week earlier in his life," Cy said. "It gave him an eye on the world to pierce the fog. I've not felt at all the same since mine. When that bag of money was dropped, I wasn't nearly as antsy as I may have been. It was like a normal event with a little twist."

"Hey, if we all had lights flash, every day might be smooth and sweet," mused Jan.

"True enough, but for unexplained reasons, only few experience it in their lives," Mark said.

"At least it's used for others more than ourselves," Cy added." A twinkling erupted in his eyes.

"A minister probably has many spiritual experiences in life. Pastor Jaba would never talk about it, though. It's personal between him and the Big Guy," said Mark.

"If it's something that would truly benefit others, he'd let the cat right out of the bag," Jan admitted "Mostly, in his sermons he'll include odd events." Jaba never talked in the Book but with it.

Cy visited a psychiatrist about his experience and was told he imagined it, but the doctor's office shook, then the whole building had cabinets, chairs and tables slam against the walls, and something else happened. A small ring of fire encircled the doctor as he sat in his chair. When he sprang up to escape, it was a whirling tornado that whisked him through the ceiling and flung him a hundred yards away. It left him seriously injured, and he questioned no more the mind of Cy or others like him.

"Are those spiritual experiences like the light bulb that flashes and illuminates the path to solve a problem?" Will asked. He flicked his laser pointer in figure eights at the ceiling.

"Like that, but it affects you stronger and far longer." Cy hesitated. "For months or years, it guides you on a path in a direction. No one makes sense of it." He felt his brain swell.

"Your mind is positive and void of negative," Mark said. "That's what you say, Dad."

"Yep, there's been more pep in my step, and all that I do

is a blast. It's often pleasure instead of the work it is. You don't know why you're exhilarated, but you are."

"Can someone else sense it if you hold or touch them, Gramps?" Jan asked. "Will it rub off, so to speak?" Cy's cranium expanded to twice its normal size and he stumbled, then stood rigid.

"I haven't tried it, so I don't know. Makes sense that it may work. W, come over here, and I'll give you a light hug for a minute," Cy prodded.

"Sure, Gramps. Think it could help my singing? As it is, I'm working hard on it, but a step ahead is welcome," Will hoped.

When Will loped toward Cy's outstretched arms, he felt like a magnet jerked his whole body, and even if he wanted to, he couldn't resist. Feeling peppery, he gawked at his arms glowing white, like a full moon in the pitch night. When he trembled, Cy grasped him and trembled, too. His face flushed and his ears popped. Then it thundered with a blinding rainbow. Will stumbled back, grinned, felt his head clear and heard crystal voices harmonize. "They must be angels," he mumbled. Hovering over him a moment were magnanimous white wings attached to gleaming faces and bodies.

"Gramps, I believe you re-re-ally have th-at magic," Will stammered. "I've never known anything like that before, but it's like a miracle."

"Maybe it'll give you more confidence," said Jan. "And have long-term effects."

"Right now, the planet is revolving around me. I can't describe what it's really like." Invisible to others, Will floated for several minutes as Jan, Cy and Mark froze like statues fixed to the floor. While he was airborne, Will grasped his arms but failed to see them. Glaring in the mirror, he was invisible! "Am I still alive or … ?" he asked, aghast at the thought. Then when he concentrated on whisking through the house, a breeze, warm and invigorating, fluttered his clothes and swept him along to the door. It creaked open and he flew upward into the clouds where he also froze. Glancing below, he noted his house shaded by the cloud nestled in a serene haven. In a few seconds there were flashes of fire that darted all around but didn't burn him. Walking on the clouds were John, Luke, Mark and Matthew, apostles of Christ. They beckoned him to come, so he did. The four stroked his cheeks, struck fear in his mind but a yearning in his heart. He sensed the coming wealth, and it would serve many in need. Then he alighted into the house to find his family speaking like nothing occurred.

"Maybe this power will help me relate to Pastor Jaba tomorrow," Cy said. "So Mark and I make a right decision about our situation. After all, it's unique." His skull had shrunk.

"You pump hands, even if he tries to hug you," Mark suggested, "to avoid zapping him with whatever you have, Dad. A stunned man gives poor advice." He swept his hands together and shook a six-inch pile of ashes onto the floor. They formed the caveat, "where the weeping willow grows, so will the mind's river flow." Weeping willows were uncommon trees, and the mind had to follow the soul's course to solve enigmas.

"Yeah, yeah. That could worsen it for us," Cy agreed. "Instead of discussing money sacks, a quick sermon on avoiding sorcery might be in order." In each of his ears, a black pearl lodged which he plucked out, eyed and pocketed. He thought of the pearl of great price. They tingled aside his thigh and mesmerized him, while visions of

Revelation swept through his mind. Heart palpitations fluttered his chest, and time halted for an instant.

"As long as Will keeps his head on so Mrs. Smith won't single him out as superior, no one there will question it, either," Jan said. Will circled fingers around his eyes in the shape of glasses.

"Hey, W, even if it is easier for you now, don't horrify the teacher," Cy warned.

"Sure, Gramps. I can control it, but I'd like it to benefit me," Will agreed. "If it hops out of the box, it'll be special."

"Make it seem you worked harder to steal the show," Mark said. "By improving each performance." Will's voice already croaked from belting notes out of his range.

"Don't concern him," Cy advised. "Besides, it may not have the same dramatic effect that it has on me, since I only transferred it to him."

"Good thinking, Dad. We're low key to reduce stress. One day at a time, as they say." Musing, he understood that this might alter his family forever. At the least, it would exorcise personal demons that may torment them.

Coon stood in the doorway to the kitchen and eyed the group. He cocked his head from side to side, as if he knew what they said. Then he sniffed the floor for crumbs, sighed and lay in the hallway.

"Keep quiet to your buddies about this," Cy said. "We don't need rumors floating that'll only agitate," he joked. "Don't try to impress a girlfriend that you can wag your tail and make her starry-eyed. This trick is for people." Coon licked his chops, moaned an 'arrh' and trotted a few circles before lying down again.

Spiritual experiences could mean many things. For some, it is getting healed of a disease they had for years. With other people, it can be when they are with family or friends, they're more at ease than when alone. With the bond they have with a pet, people may experience it. Most love their animals, and they may seem like part of themselves sometimes. Coon and Cy bond, except Cy loves his family more. He cherishes Will, and he sees him as himself when he was a boy. Mark and Jan are his other two loves. When we're on a high and don't know why, it may be a spiritual experience that carries you away from worry and problems. God is there at these times, beside us.

Lacking spiritual experiences doesn't assure a harsh life, but some hardships may linger, and prayer may bring slower answers. When it's answered, more doubt could arise as to its benefit. But those are only maybes, not certain. Look to the soul then. The McGinns view life dissimilar from many in Greentown. They've stumbled upon a wealth of money and are at odds what to do with it. There was liberty before it. After it wound their path, they spent over a month bewildered. With work, the puzzle may assemble.

CHAPTER 21

"Who wants to finish the pot?" Jan asked. "Of course, it means washing dishes tonight, too." Coon crept up to her and snatched the pot from her hand, then lapped his wide tongue around inside to clean it out. "Thanks for washing it," Jan quipped.

"I'll help anyway," Mark offered, "to keep my thoughts positive. For the pastor, Dad will write questions and likely responses. And you, Mr. Talent," he said to Will, "continue your school tasks until completion."

Slapping his CD headphones on, Will blanked Mark out. "In my mind, I'll work the music into all else. That means spending most time on it," Will resisted.

"If I find any other grades lacking, we'll yank you from your love until they go to the top," Mark snapped.

"Should I fail to reach my goals, you'll be partially to blame. So I'll live solo."

"You're not affecting me if you do that but your friends and maybe future, so think."

"Dad, I'm not disappointing myself or others. My fire is full time, but music's first forever." He pumped his fist.

Jan was sure Will was going to make music his life. "That's a winner, son," Jan said. "Never give up or give in, and believe you will do it. Not can do it."

"Mark, we'll work some tonight as well," Cy suggested. "Two heads beat one. It'll take thought, prayer and reading the Book. We've never been up close to that much money before and likely never will again. For some people it's a dream, though. Or a nightmare."

"I've got it, Dad. As soon as I'm done we'll get it going. The meeting will solve what we're dealing with," Mark agreed.

"I'm going to work on my science project," Will said. "After that, before my music, the rest of the subjects get attention. Then it will get all the rehearsal it needs." The project was to prove that lesser gravity on earth would yield more century life spans.

Will knew that he'd slap his headphones on, flip a CD into the player and go for the gusto while he did the boring tasks. The tunes would track in his mind so that he'd analyze every chord, lyric, melody and chorus to memorize them. His goal was to live and breathe music, and his heart and soul were already there, riding the wind. On to fame and fortune the gust would sweep him, but it would be years, maybe not by the eighteen that he dreamed of. Gramps shelved his chance; it wasn't happening to him.

"If you need to use the studio, you can, Will," Jan said. "Your dad and Gramps are done with their new home plans and will be a while on their situation." She flipped her hands and rolled her eyes.

"Hope you and Gramps get that money sack to the owner," Will said. "I'm glad you know how to deal with it. I sure wouldn't." He'd pocket it to do his first world tour.

"On the rise is more trouble," Cy feared. "Not our trouble, though."

"We won't concern ourselves if it's vanished, and that's possible," Mark hoped. He had no intention of slipping by it or refusing it.

"Don't be up late guys," Jan warned. "For me tomorrow is critical, since I'll be taking over the program for a month. So I'm resting early." She'd one day begin her own company to teach women management skills.

"We'll only be a bit, then we'll rest, too, so we'll be on time for Pastor Jaba," Cy said.

Cy and Mark shuffled to the living room, slipping a few chairs to the round table, feeling like King Arthur and Sir Lancelot before a major battle. "We'll keep it brief, with the facts," Mark said. "He's not an investigator but a minister with wisdom." If Jaba balked at them, he and Cy would walk and do a search.

"Good suggestion. But he'll ride with us and see the sack. The Chinese said that a picture is worth a thousand words, and the real view is priceless."

"That's a good option, but we chat him up so his mind, not emotions, turns ideas over." He felt the heat of the SWAT, FBI and ATF broiling his skin.

"Yes, even a preacher's eyes may dance if millions of dollars face them," Cy responded. In his own eyes a gleam sensed a better life. The McGinns knew their options. If they worked it themselves the cash could be theirs. No need to deal with Jaba in case he wasn't wise, called the newspaper to implicate them in a plot to horde the fortune and ruined them. He debated which direction to go.

They knew Pastor Jaba was totally honest, but he led a small church, and to keep it going he craved money. Mark and Cy read about Chile and knew that it was a poor South American country. The people were simple but likely hungry. Pastor was saddened by that, and the memories of where he came from could affect how he'd react to a windfall of money. He loved children, and was especially struck by poverty, whether in Chile or the U.S. In Chile he'd begun an orphanage and wanted one here. Each child should feel like someone cared and loved them. So Mark realized the pastor's purpose for a large sum of money.

"Likely, he'd see it in terms of offerings for years instead of the world's value of it," Mark felt. "That's pure, assisting others with a windfall, instead of seeing a bigger house, new car, vacations all over."

"Few of us could say, 'I'll save so much of that for a snowy day,'" Cy said.

"After enjoying some life, buying an island, selling sea-shells with the newfound wealth, we'd save most of it," Mark admitted. He kneaded his hands in anticipation.

Visualizing the money sacks again Cy agreed, "That's our goal, saving it."

Mark and Jan knew that they scoured for presents for each other's birthdays and Will's. But stores weren't places to hang out. There were going out to movies, parks and taking long drives from state to state on weekends and holidays. The beauty of mountains in Colorado, Utah, Wyoming and New Mexico; the Washington monument; going to the Midwest to see snow in winter beckoned them. At one time they were caught in a blizzard. When they were about to starve, an older couple whipped by their snow-laden car, buried but for a tail light, and screeched in front of them. The husband rushed from the car, then his wife. They scratched through to the window and asked if they were okay. The McGinns moaned, "No, we're freezing to death." The couple brought them food, hot tea and coffee, took them to a hotel and paid for their stay. It was enlightening. The Good Samaritan all over.

"There are few stores in Greentown. Don't need 'em. And you know why," Cy offered. "Only the best quality will do here. A century ago that's how the town got its name."

CHAPTER 22

"I remember, Dad, that Mayor Primo gawked when 'Christmas Carol' was performed at the playhouse," Mark said.

"He was going to be certain that no man, woman or child would suffer the way Tiny Tim did. Sickening," Cy snapped. "When a guy called Scrooge was married to his money, there was a child who barely survived. Until the old rich guy saw those three ghosts of Christmas past, present and future, Tim's family suffered."

"Oh, Dad, and the clincher was that when Ebenezer saw his tombstone, he knew that his money wasn't going with him. Then, my, did his hardened heart flow. Not only did Tiny Tim get the operation that he needed to heal his crippled legs, Bob Cratchet, his dad, got a huge pay raise, the family got the best meal that they ever had at Christmas, and Scrooge saw light each day."

"Every family is pushed to vote by Primo's great grandchildren, and notices are sent out to all on who is going to keep the 'this is the best place anywhere' work going. Primo grew up with parents who abused him and his brother. Eliza and Guthrie withheld food and clothing, making them earn them at age ten. On the street they hawked newspapers, apples and collectibles for them. That was before their grandma jerked Primo's parents, her children, into a back room and bolted them in until they begged and assured they'd only have the kids work part time for allowances," Cy said.

"Guys," Jan added, as she popped into the room and onto the couch, "also, we don't tolerate mistreating others in any way. Each person controls his or herself so that we see more kindness here. Who would want it any other way?" Their hospital trauma unit was rife with victims from other locales. There had been a few assaults and murders, but they were years ago.

"Not I," Cy and Mark said in unison. "If someone gave each of us a full money sack to leave, we'd pass on being happily rich for being happy."

"The saying is older than all of us together; money alone can't buy happiness," Jan said. When she got donors to give each of her girls a thousand dollars, they returned most of what they bought with it. When they threw the rest in the bank for college, they enrolled, and most graduated to lead better lives.

"Oh, you may not think about living costs, but it can't make you happy only for its sake," Mark knew. But it would ease his own angst over life's uncertainties.

Many of those with more money, even the rich, may be unfulfilled. For them to laugh and smile or even enjoy gifts like sunrises and sunsets can be challenging. To protect their money takes quite a lot of energy and joy. Then there are average people who delight in the little they have. Having more money makes some things easier in life, like buying a car, a house and traveling, fewer worries paying bills. Cy and Mark eyed a garden of cash. As they debate what to do, no longer average persons, they'll grasp a new reality.

"Only when you provide for others; there's warmth inside and out every time," Cy said. Grinning as he said this, he stroked his chin and batted his eyes.

"If the money we're seeing at Doc's is oddly unclaimed, and we get it, we'd begin a unique charity," Mark suggested. "That's the thrill of the heart. There's little to match it."

"Yes, because it'll reward us and others," Jan added. "I'm sure even Will can suggest purposes." She also knew he'd get himself suits, equipment and gigs.

"Most young people can create ways to improve the world," Cy realized. "Give them a chance, and the wonders are many." Giving them too much strangles success.

"When the desire to spend is removed and kids use money with thought, near-miracles occur," Jan believed. "Dad gave me an allowance, but Mom gave me no extra money. When I saved for goals, I grew. On my first job I learned that you lose your time, not only money, if you waste a penny." Her grandfather had been a baron with a castle, land and millions of Swiss francs but passed only thousands to her parents and much to his servants.

CHAPTER 23

"People successful with money and jobs respect them," Mark understood. "Not everyone constantly searches for all that's greener." Green and gold may look the same, with the green being visions of happiness and a large amount of money being the method that some people believe can buy their way to it.

"It used to be, 'look before you leap,' but any leap requires a lot of looks. Then look back at where you're leaving. Is it that bad, or did you tell yourself that?" Cy asked.

"Yes, Gramps. The people who do well think on their own in order," Jan said. "The unwise see results before costs, so are leapers, not lookers."

"If you don't think first, you can't be a winner," Mark assured.

"Usually it's the mistake, not the right that's noticed," Cy said.

Cy remembered his first time in a recording studio.

He crossed a few of the wires and got the amplifier confused with the song mixing board. There was a horrendous squeal, a crack, and the equipment smoked and blew its electronics. Outside in the field he dashed to hide under the biggest bush there until the crew promised not to chase him and flail the stars out of him. They squeezed it out of his wages, and he hungered for nearly a month. Then he studied the manuals until he could repair most of it.

"Hey Dad and Gramps," boasted Will, who had heard them from his room and popped in, "my performance is so clean that no one will see the fault if I make one. That's what rehearsals are for. Once it's part of you, you won't blow it when you're before the public. I won't be ridiculed because I didn't do my job." Before him he saw the great stage where he bowed and heard the audience applaud for more. From the proscenium he hurtled into them by a swinging chandelier and tumbled into a seat beside his wife. She glanced at him and mouthed a silent 'you're my hero' then swirled into a pyramid of stars. The pyramid flashed onto a dollar bill that became hundreds and millions. He felt this predicted that his wife would be his reason for success.

"Right, W, most people see no sweat in a local theatre performance. Behind the scenes, they'd be baffled but would honor a performer who committed even a major error on stage. They'd allow a quiet time for him or her to recover so the work could go on smoothly. It's getting on the platform," Gramps believed.

At the door was a knock. It was Sally Lu, who struggled learning her lines. Cy answered the door. "Hi Sally, what's wrong?" He knew by her sullen face.

"Gramps, I'm not ready for the play. No matter how long I study, the words stick briefly and disappear." Her blue eyes were streaked red and her white hair was mussed.

"Will, come here. This young lady needs your skills. Explain those tricks you know from your efforts." Will straggled to her and clasped her hand.

"First you relax for a few minutes, close your eyes and take several deep breaths," Will said and watched Sally do this and followed her in the motions. "Now open your eyes and glance at this script. Pretend you're adding one plus one or learning your ABC's. Look at only the first few lines of your part." Her glazed eyes scanned them, then she sighed.

"You make it look so easy, because for you it is. We don't learn like you, Will. Maybe I should let another girl have my part. That's what I can do." She frowned and blushed.

"Before you do that, I'll quit the play, and it's not happening. Listen, you need to come by daily, and we'll rehearse. Through a few lines at a time I'll guide you, showing you techniques to succeed. We'll enjoy and it won't be like work. You'll see. When you get through a page, think of a reward, and I'll have Gramps grasp your arm so you can live your reward. He has this gift ... I've said too much. Anyway, he makes it seem like your birthday, Christmas and many favorite events rolled into one."

"It's critical that you believe in yourself first, Sally, then I can work that magic that has benefited us for a while now. It's spiritual and takes that mustard seed faith to occur. Do you know what I mean, miss?" Cy asked as his eyes twinkled, his face glowed red, then white, and he levitated three feet into the air before floating to the floor.

"Yes, Gramps. I can do what I think I can," Sally believed, as her eyes popped, then into the air she rose, felt a great weight leave her and swept into a fluorescent yellow mist that veiled her from view and vanished after it swarmed her mind with a sense of ease that she'd never known. She whizzed through her lines after Will worked with her again. "Thanks, Gramps," she squealed, then pounced to hug him and give him a quick buss on his cheek. "Will, I can't wait to get on that stage now. Maybe I'll be leading lady! See you soon," she said, patted Coon and skipped her way out the door.

Mark continued. "Sally and Will are ready now, but Dad, if you had stayed in the business, on your hiatus you could've taught me all you know and, who knows, we may have begun our own recording studio to compete with major ones that have been around fifty years. C&M Productions is what we'd have called it."

"Greentown would have been the biggest little place in the country. The mayor would have approved us for a tourist stop. A quick roll-through a few times a day by small vans wouldn't affect our quiet," Jan said. Then she saw big RVs and shut her eyes. In her heart she was ambivalent about the excess attention a tourist attraction would draw.

"True," Mark agreed. "A small-scale attraction that brings a few people is okay. We would teach visitors about recording, not show the glory of those who 'made it' due to our work. It could have been thrilling." In his mind were the flash of neon lights and the clamor of visitors inquiring about their business. He was queasy from the thoughts.

Mark decided that they would have a studio if they were awarded much of the money in the sack. They'd begin by giving top groups and singers free studio time to earn a name for themselves. Then there would be battles of the bands to draw crowds and respect for them all over Georgia and later, the whole U.S.

"Yeah, cracking jokes is how we'd have taught them. There's nothing like funny to crackle your cranium and get you to remember how to learn music. Mrs. Smith has us laughing, and we sweep the lessons and rehearsal," Will said.

"When we used to do that," Cy admitted, "it might snowball so we'd get behind on a session. We'd be strict the rest of the week, or it could be damaging to the artist, sometimes Elvis, who had concerts after finishing a record. Have humor to keep interest in what you love." On his face was a deadpan grin that divulged his professional nature.

Laughing and cracking jokes is better than being serious all the time. Too many people lose their desire for humor when things disturb them. Do something to laugh and enjoy yourself. Read a funny book, watch a goofy movie or join others who make you laugh. There are few ways to feel better. Think about anything amusing that has happened, and make yourself cackle about it. To do this may take a while, but it can really help weather brutish times. Not everyone does this as well as they want to. But if you focus you can. Take time to practice it, and things should feel better if it's hard for them to be better. There is enough to fret. Be happy by seeking the humor in life. When something irks you, clip it off and flutter after. This may soften the burden.

"One of the best gifts," Mark felt, "is to have humorous friends. Hunt for them and keep them. Call and see them when you're up or down. Let them lean on you."

CHAPTER 24

"Humor is useful in all parts of life," Jan said. "More of our women get on track and succeed with that spice to improve their outlook. Very few fail to respond to humor, and most go home or to work more elated than morose. Plus, they know that we care and love them. Nothing surpasses that," she gushed. Her face screwed up and her eyes squinted as the thought of a better life coursed through her mind.

"But look at all aggrieved, and it's like the worst disease on earth. Masses scatter from that situation. Never are only a few affected. They're all over," Mark added.

"Meeting one positive person a day makes life so grand," Cy said. "Perhaps we need a local comedy club." Cy could still do a vaudeville act, as he had done some work with George Burns when he was working at RCA with Elvis. He'd even been taught some dance steps by Fred Astair, one of the early greats of that talent.

"It takes a gift to make most people rejoice. Bob Hope,

George Burns and Robin Williams are some talented ones I think of," offered Mark. "A rapid way to get humor is to read the comics daily. Listen to some of those around you." Even in the Greentown newspaper, comics are what he'd turn to first. Then he may watch a kid's cartoon after he arrived from work.

"People of comedy had pain before," Jan knew. "It's often the low times in their lives that they reverse to make us laugh. It doesn't only start as the joke they hear in their minds. Humorists seldom come from wealthy families. Through their travails, they devise ways to take them, add some ingredients and develop jokes that bring joy."

"Yes, but when someone cranks our minds upward, we all benefit from it," Mark knew.

"There's enough negative in America to be removed by the funny people. That's why we pretend there's no TV but an hour a day," Cy realized.

"Few who begin in comedy make it to the top. You have to know people so well, why they laugh," Mark said.

"People are complex." Cy had worked with hundreds. "They think of humor for different reasons. Jewish, military, younger and older are more likely to snicker at jokes that apply to their group."

"If people know the humorist quite well, he or she can use events that could offend some," Jan said. "Bob Hope belittled many of the U.S. presidents, but they'd only smirk in return or respond with a witty remark of their own. And Mark Twain could gaffe with late-night talk-show hosts."

"A performer in music has to please all of the fans," Will knew. "No matter what, you have to sing to them all." Those who read people well can become excellent creators. Will heard several of the groups of recent years: Journey, Metallica, Aerosmith, AC-DC. His style wasn't to be hard rock, but pop rock. His ears and mind were attuned to a larger group of fans to please. He felt his career longevity depended upon selecting soft popular music or a blend of blues, popular, classic and folk. A favorite was John Denver's style, especially "Country Roads."

"Yeah," Cy agreed. "When you glance at them, their mood stirs a while. Many singers must perform through dance and body gestures. If it appeals to the audience, they do it, regardless of other opinions."

"Music is a gift meant for others. Artists reward themselves by offering the gift," Mark added. Performance is critical for artist success. Unless the singer's style is such that performance like dance or extra bodily movements are not necessary, like Celine Dion, a choreographer who trains in dance movements is usually needed.

"It's not only the money singers make, it's the song and the love the singer feels that make their lives," Jan said. "Many people in jobs drudge through their feelings about them to earn a living."

"If I have to, I'll give a few performances for free, then others will want to pay for it," Will felt. "Some have had to do that." He had heard of only a few who allowed free samples of their talents for display before succeeding.

"Creative people, in acting or music, love their work like themselves. To make them 'live' in a way that the readers cherish, writers must feel the characters in their book." Cy had read hundreds of books before he was twenty. The best writers read widely and remember scene, dialogue and plot.

By writing a journal of how they feel each day, anyone can begin creating what happened and then make characters, stories or songs out of it. Cy and Will see the world in a similar way. Music makes them mellow and flow through life. Cy may saw wood but is going to make sure that Will sings into a career where he loves what he does.

For others to buy it, your work must please you first. He knew that those who began young at a goal were more likely to achieve it. A focus on one work at a time, then the step up to others when successful, was the correct path. Will couldn't ascend the mountain without scaling the foothills.

"That's how anyone creates, though, Dad," Mark offered. "Like Charles Schulz who drew the Peanuts comic strip or Jim Davis who does Garfield. They always imagined ideas for the characters of their strips or used daily experiences with a twist."

"Oh, they may use their own lives to put similar events in the comic," Cy said.

"And that works," Jan said. "Charles Schulz wasn't the popular kid in school, so Charlie Brown was the fall guy for Lucy's stunts of pulling the football off the ground when he was going to kick off. Then he'd flip over onto the ground when he kicked at the air in its place." Drawing humor takes two talents, art and communication.

"Oh, that was a favorite, but all his comics were good," Mark grinned. "He was rare. For him to be popular for fifty years is unique. In many creative fields, few people do well longer than ten years."

"Every day of the week he worked drawing and adding talk lines," Jan said. "He labored with love until illness prevented his doing so before he passed." It was said he made twelve million dollars a month at his death. That income is extremely unusual for the creative person, however.

"It was really a labor of his soul," suggested Cy. "I remember the early strip. It was simple. Later ones were more complex and the characters appeared more realistic."

"He was enamored with the big little kids of his world. They were like his real family, and people knew them," Mark knew. Charles had a real family, of course, a wife, two sons, and a daughter. He never neglected them due to his work but honored them with his time.

There was Snoopy, Charlie's beagle; Woodstock, the yellow bird friend of Snoopy's; Linus, Lucy's brother who had his security blanket but was quite bright; Sally, Charlie's sister; Lucy, who took advantage of Charlie; Schroeder, who played Beethoven on his piano; Peppermint Pattie, the freckled friend of Charlie's; Marcy, the bespectacled friend of Peppermint Pattie's and Pigpen, whose every move swished a cloud of dust around, as he hated the water.

"It was a better family, since they were close in so many ways," Jan observed.

"Creating a comic is a short story read in minutes," Cy said. "The reader has to beam once the story ends."

Laughing is one of the few ways to deal with life, even when it disturbs you. Let's watch something soul feeding, such as cartoons, comedy TV show or movies. Instead of being sad, gag at humor. It may even make cloudy days seem sunny and warm. If you go to school, dwell upon a friend's jokes or when you get home and can do what you enjoy. Listen to music, play games in or outside, draw, write, go over to a friend's house or have them come over to talk and enjoy life. It can be flying a kite, playing a musical instrument, goofing off or seeing yourself as funny. Make up jokes and try them out on friends or parents. Write songs, stories and poems or write personal thought feelings and daily events in a journal. Do what you love. Share it with friends or family when you can—or a pet.

When school, events of the world, family tiffs or any personal problems begin to disturb you, pray how to deal with it, ask for a positive mind, plead for humor and strength to wade through it. Then use what you love to rise on your higher heart.

CHAPTER 25

"In a song, it's the chorus that makes it great. The singer and writer know that," Will knew. The hook of a song must occur within the first thirty seconds. The hook is the repeated part of the chorus or those words that stick in our memory long after we've listened to the song. It is actually part of the chorus or the words in the song repeated most often. In the Elvis song "Marie's the name of his latest flame" is the hook.

"Like 'Marie's the name of his latest flame' in Elvis' song," Cy added. "It's hard to forget that chorus," and he wept with lips pursed as the song and studio days drilled his mind. He thought of a later song that he loved by a group that began in the sixties, The Beatles. It was "The Long and Winding Road." Even at his age, he believed that the songs of the mid-sixties and early seventies were the best. One singer he thought of now, who is known for his amazing guitar work is B.B. King, a black blues singer.

He even named his guitar Lucille. It's his leading lady, and she knows how to cater to anyone able to listen to her.

"It's near 11 o'clock, so who has to talk with the pastor tomorrow?" Jan asked. She stood with arms akimbo, wagging her head between her men and tapping her foot. "Come on, let's roll. Providence prefers no delays."

"I guess one of us, so it's important to get rest, wouldn't you say, Dad?" Mark asked.

"We're heading that way," Cy agreed. He hesitated at his door to eye Coon on the bed.

"How are you on the homework?" Jan queried Will. "Since you were chiming in here so much, I presume you were done." She recalled how she would muse about anything but homework for an hour after she returned home from school. Her dream was to be a prima ballerina, performing in Tchaikovsky's "Nutcracker Suite." Dance she did, in her room, the yard and on stage up through high school. But her college years were lean times, and she set the dream aside for the near future. Seeking a scholarship, she was barely nudged out by a friend by only a few points in a recital. Her first love she would pursue, but later.

"I finished early tonight," Will admitted. "It just flowed better, so I thought maybe it was Gramps' touch that did it. It was natural to do, and that included the rehearsal songs."

"Then this could be a real gift to us all. When we have a problem, Gramps caresses us for a minute and it disappears. Don't divulge it to anyone else, though," Jan warned. She squinted her eyes and glared at her men. "It's not a miracle to be penned by the press or blogged about on the Web. Someone might even kidnap Cy to find out how they could cop a piece of the action."

"No one would believe it anyway," Mark moaned. "They'd say we're whacked."

"I didn't plan on making something out of it. Not a good idea," Cy snapped.

"Right, we have Cy's help only when a problem is unbearable," Jan said. Much of life was unbearable to the people. Only through prayer, powerful family support and joyous communications was their life better than many.

"Whenever you have a gift, don't abuse it. There's a reason that you were given it and not someone else," Will offered.

"That's true, son. Some might use it only for themselves. A good heart may turn sour on us," Jan agreed. She sighed at her girls' high divorce rate.

Jan felt what some of her girls did some days, and she knew that it was easier to grovel rather than work at solutions. If she meditated, prayed or read a good book to sideline problems or solve them, it made her jovial.

"Likely, I'd even forget I could do whatever it is if I weren't reminded of it by those who feel it's a big deal. It can be for those who need it. I'm more spry than I was at twenty, and the world flocks to one who would enlighten them," Cy said.

"I'm glad Gramps didn't make me feel too juvenile," Will added. "Like a baby whining constantly. Fortunately, he clarified my thinking—it's more rapid and my memory's better." In ten minutes he learned what had taken him an hour. Then he gleaned wisdom from novellas and biographies, including classic works.

"That's it, though," suggested Mark. "We get only what we need. Otherwise, it makes us jaded. Dad is invaluable to society now, not only the family. Of course, we conceal it until we must tell others. That is, unless he wants to reach the world."

"Thanks all of you, for honoring this gift," Cy praised.

"In some families, oh, there would have been fireworks. A few are nervy about what others think, one may want me on TV to talk with Oprah or Letterman, and maybe another hordes it when he plum wants to fly every second." He twiddled his two hairs and scowled.

"Hey Dad, that's right," Mark agreed.

"If I didn't have to rehearse or study, my friends, even Shannon and Sally Lu, would ostracize me too," Will said. His face screwed up and flushed at the thought.

Cy felt eccentric about his power, like a magician. Applying it wrongly might bring a curse upon him. Thinking about it, he wondered when he should use it, or if it could be controlled. When he fingered his head, even he was exhilarated. But should he rejuvenate at will? That he didn't know. It was something he'd examine before he served others. The sun shone daily now, and he felt no anguish. That was unprecedented. But he yearned to undergo a gamut of emotions, didn't he? Or he might fail to sense how others lived. When he eyed the world, he fretted not and guffawed at anything. It was marvelous to be like this; others would experience it, too.

Cy crooned songs from early days and perused amusing stories. When he reflected on amusing events, he cackled about them, too. There were some incidents that quelled his mirth, like tragedies, and it depressed him. Once he dwelled upon the pleasant, he could only grin. It was life full of exhilaration.

"I'll assure it's not just a Mr. Fix It program," Cy chirped. "This is to assist people, not allow them to forget themselves, for sure. I trust that living with it will lift others first." It was a spiritual gift, like Jesus' healing millennia ago. He'd offer it with wisdom.

"Gramps, avoid donating it to those with immoral

motives," Jan warned. "It's too easy for you to falter and allow it into the wrong hands. Disaster."

"It's time to prepare for tomorrow, though," Cy reminded. "Pastor Jaba anticipates us. I trust that he won't grill us about what we can't answer. Ministers may do that."

"Sure Dad," Mark agreed. "A third mind will ease the solution for the odd situation."

"Keep rolling on, son," Jan interrupted. "We'll expect a grand opening on Broadway one of these years. But for now, hope to hear your name announced first or second on the Greentown Middle School Theatre brochure. That'll do." Jan knew that success as a child was no guarantee Will would make it in the music as an adult, but he would strive.

"In about a month, the play date will be on, Mom," Will offered. "You'll get a letter from Mrs. Smith, as the school always notifies everyone. Each of us gets four guest tickets, at no cost, so most families can go. What benefits! Sometimes the roles are changed at the last week, which could make it almost impossible for me to be in the play. So don't get your hopes too high. If it's meant to be, it'll happen. Once we think positive, it will eventually work out but may take time."

"If you don't make it after all, you'll have to plod through future rehearsals to try again. But if you do, the extra tickets are going to my girls who need recreation in their lives," said Jan. Her clients were tense and had little income to go to the local movie every few months. The money went mostly for living. She knew they were meant to have a total life.

"We'll all have a good day tomorrow. Rest well," Mark sang as he climbed the stairs to their room. "Hurry up, Jan. For us to be early, we need to keep a tight schedule."

"Be there in a few," Jan responded, flipping off the switches before following.

When they reached the room, there was a brief discussion about Will's future and Cy's relationship with him. "We have to use caution in our encouragement of Will, and Gramps dwelling on his past that was not successful won't help matters any," Jan said, sitting on the edge of their king-size bed with lavender sheets adorning it and gold-threaded brocade on its perimeter.

"We're both partners in advocating his obsessive nature regarding his future in the performing arts. We need to send him to voice training and a private performance academy in addition to public auditions so he gets a taste of rejection. It may make him grow or condition his mind to accept loss in life. If not, it may damage him later," Mark said, wiggling his leg in a nervous twitch. His eyes twinkled, as he believed in positive thoughts for his son, but he wrung his hands as he sensed reality was waiting to snare the unwary.

"Maybe Cy should be discouraged from that Elvis routine. He was a phenomenon, rare in the best of all worlds. Look at the rejections on American Idol. Those youth are traumatized by that. If Will heeds it, his life would have a better track, and priorities could be understood. We'll support him for now, though." She sighed, and beads of sweat swept across her cheeks onto the parquet floor. "Let's discuss it more later, if necessary, and sleep."

"Right, but we keep a vigil for any problems in the family."

CHAPTER 26

"Yep, water and food dish okay," Cy noted for Coon, then he tumbled into bed.

"Night, Gramps," Will said before patting Coon and turning in.

"Dream well W," Cy answered. He lay, eyed the ceiling and slumbered. As he tossed and turned a bit, he thought his wife called. Was he awake? Heeding the voice, he mumbled, "Yes, love, I know. It's been years. In the house, felt alone, so Will wanted me here. He needed Gramps to fill the family, loves his mom and dad but thought me deserted at the old place. I'm not sure. Yeah, I'll be here more now. Won't sell the house. I want it to work out okay. Coon? He likes it, too. He's at home here while we're at work. Will's back early. Yes, W still remembers your birthday. A bit odd; he buys and wraps you a gift for the tree each Christmas. Okay, no problem. This spring and summer I'll care for the garden. Bye, dear. I know it's wonderful up there. See you when I'm called. Love you. Take care." He dozed again. Coon had heard him, clicked into the room, eyed Cy sleeping and slumped at the head of his bed. In response to Cy's voice he sighed.

Dawn shimmered, blanketing the mellow late winter morning sun through Cy's triangular picture window. It failed to awaken him for moments, but Coon would. He tossed aside from a beam of light creeping across his eyes. As something warm and wet brushed his forehead, he started. It was Coon bestowing his special wake-up call. At first, Cy shoved him aside, sensing he disturbed his reverie. Then he cradled his neck and bussed his furred skull. Coon's ears flickered in response.

"Okay, hold on buddy," Cy whispered. "No one else is stirring yet, so we'll wait a short time to get going here." He eyed Coon prancing out toward his food dish. "A sweet fellow," Cy added. Coon cocked his head to offer a conciliatory wink of his left eye.

A whistle he thought was Mark's was Will's as he crept to the restroom. In a half hour was normal wake up. Coon straggled back and laid his head at the foot of the bed.

"You sure do quicken the heart, amigo," Cy said. "I don't know what we did before we had dogs to soothe us. Mumbled to ourselves too much, probably. With you at home the nights were tolerable. More of us elders need you, since the youth have each other. Their pets may not get the attention that we give you. When we return you're there to greet us. Never too busy to show us how much you love us. Too bad humans aren't always that way, but life is too swift and impersonal. If we learned from you, it would be so rosy."

Coon arose, pranced to Cy and set his jaw on his cheek, resting it there so that he felt his warm fur and wet nose.

Then Coon dripped something small and cool. Only rarely had he done it, but he cried because he loved Cy so and always would.

"That makes me think there's a bit of human in all of you. When you grieve or are afflicted in the heart, you do what we would. It's the oddest emotion for an animal to show, but you do and we cherish you for it," Cy said.

Cy couldn't imagine life without his old friend. He was a companion when Maggie was alive, and she doted on him, petting him when Cy couldn't and massaging his aches. Almost everywhere he followed. At the beach, he barked to the lifeguard and saved a drowning swimmer, then was awarded a citizenship medal for it. Going to the mountains, he opposed a black bear that Maggie and Cy didn't see until it was almost upon them. With a snarl that would threaten a rhinoceros, he drove it back to the woods. Once Cy dozed while driving the Packard. A nip on the chest and a head nudge awakened him. The proudest he made Cy was when he contended with a pit bull dog only a foot away from slashing a chunk from Maggie's leg. Coon lunged at the dog, snapped his throat and slung him as he scampered off with a whimper. Yes, it was some dog he had.

Although Coon had snatched the family's food before, he honored them otherwise. He scampered their shoes to them or bounded on them, smothering them with kisses. Sometimes he'd lay beside them and peer at them, begging forgiveness. It was always a way they'd remember.

"Hey Gramps," Jan sniffed, ducking her head into the doorway. "It's hotcakes today, so you're extra sweet for the preacher. And they're our Friday favorite."

"Every week's too much. Try some French toast next time. I think Mark likes them better, too. We'll tolerate them today," he sighed. "But will be there shortly, ma'am,"

Cy chirped. "I'm going to wash my sleepy eyes first, so I'll be wide awake." He glanced at himself in the mirror, combed his two hairs and yawned.

"Since you've moved in, there've been no complaints. I trust you're not getting ill," Sal said. "Take your time, Gramps. You know that the buttermilk, pecans, nutmeg and cinnamon must be mixed well. Or Will rushes in here to remind me of the recipe. He'll snap at me like a mad dog, so I don't test him," Jan sighed.

"Ever thought about submitting that to Pillsbury for their semi-annual Bake-Off contest?" Cy suggested. "I read that the top prize is up to $1,000,000 now. All you have to do is use one of their products, like the Dough Boy. Only kidding. Really, it is their dough or pancake mix you have to use, though. Or their other products to make the recipe with, and then submit it according to the rules."

"They're not that good. But if I get a chance one day, it's a thought. Maybe with your confidence you could enter the contest," Jan admitted. "Call them Jan and Cy's Sweetcakes."

"Sure, next time they have entries, we'll give it a go. You can't lose anything by trying, only by not attempting it at all," Cy said brusquely. He wasn't after the money but the honor that came with the award. Honor first above all was his moral belief.

Cy recalled his mother. What a match that was, with his dad Scottish and his mom Swiss. In the Scottish highlands, she detested the rains for months, and he flopped on his face or tumbled into the nearest grove of trees when he donned skis in Switzerland. But as he got the hang of it, he snatched their cat, Zita, tossing her into his backpack with only her head bobbing out, then zipped down the mountain as the cat clawed her way out. That was the last time he treated a cat like a dog, as it hung its claws into his stomach all the way down. Even after offering her the best cat treats, the animal sunk its teeth into his nose as soon as he attempted to make amends by facing down and begging the cause.

"I heard that, Mom," snapped Will. "Remember that great-grandma Svetlana from Switzerland taught you the skills. Think before you let the whole world have them," he reminded. "I'd have to lock you up." He glared at Jan and felt betrayed. It was something he concealed from all and would pass on to his children.

"Yes, the family name is worth more than gold, and I'm sure that Dad and Gramps thought about it with the big sack of green they may see again today, right?" Jan asked sardonically. She tossed her head back with aplomb.

"Of course," Mark boomed from the hallway, still waving the hairdryer along his tousled curls. "Average people dream about what happened to us, no matter where the cash came from. Oh, they'd debate how to spend it. But if they felt they could hide it to keep—for the good life, few would leave it alone, walk away and ask a religious authority what to do with it. We're definitely different. But honest."

"Then what are we going to do with it if some odd situation allows us to keep most or all of it?" Will asked. "Still live in Greentown or at a beach house? Having it and using it can conflict. Plus, charities need money." He envisioned surfboards and sand.

"The only thing we're sure about now," said Mark, "is that it's not our money and we don't know its source." Musing how wealthy athletes, entertainers and CEO's got to live, he wanted to live like that, too, so he'd accept the money if it were legally allotted to him rather than refuse it. But it rattled his mind as he slept, so that each day brought more distress about their involvement. His reliance on divine guidance is all that saved him.

"But within the next few days we'll know," Cy admitted. "It may be that a reward's attached for its recovery. That's often the case when large sums of money are missing."

"That can be generous, in the high thousands for large finds. But we don't need an incentive to report it," Jan added. "Getting greedy for even small amounts can turn on you."

"Honesty rewards itself and avoids the bad news press, too," Cy agreed. "Even old Coon has whisked up purses ladies dropped and rushed to return them. One grateful older lady paid thousands of dollars for his food and vet bills. Her husband had owned a family business that he sold after fifty years to one of the biggest companies in America. She cackled and said, 'Plenty of honest people I've met, but only one trusty dog. Thank you sir, and treat him like a king's pet for me.'"

"Good story, Gramps," Will chirped. "Maybe Coon could be an example for kids when they find others' property. There've been petty thefts in school and in the halls now are security guards," he scowled. A number of times, as a witness, he reported the scofflaw. Offered a reward, he refused it. His reward was an enlightened heart that thumped with pride.

"Animals can't be dishonest," Jan said. "Instinct controls what they do, and they don't think about how a find benefits them but know it goes back to who lost it. Simple."

"When there are no 'what ifs' to change minds, most people are honest. When no thoughts of the luxury if you're better off, not having to work, no money worries ever again come up," said Mark. He didn't require church to imbed his values, as Cy and Maggie had lit his honorable path in life due to their spirituality.

It was odd how Coon had returned the lady's purse. He was an intelligent dog, but it was amazing that he'd find the purse on the ground, then prance to the lady who owned it. They could see it now. In a store window a grandma with glasses whose husband left his account eyes merchandise. She rummages in her purse with thousands of dollars and thinks to save it all for her house full of cats. While she's out, they're home meowing like sirens for her to return. She dwells upon their meowing at the house and spins around to go home. Her purse drops when she sees a strange dog that scares her. Coon was spooked by himself in the mirror, but he rambles toward her, and she scatters from him. Then he snags her purse and barks for attention. Grinning, the grandmother straggles to Coon, kisses him, and is lapped silly. Yes, sir, dogs are usually honest, even if a grandmother wipes her face as thanks.

CHAPTER 27

"Well, it's about an hour before the bus for you, sir," Jan said to Will.

"Then there's no rush, Mom. Quit being so stressed in the morning, as it gets under our skin. Rushing food down is unhealthy," he chided her. She frowned at him.

"And it's making my two hairs stand on end to consider it," Cy grunted as he swallowed his last drop of coffee. "But guess I'll add to the nerves, because I need another cup of java, please. With more butter cream and honey, Jan."

"To go with it are the first two pancakes off the griddle, Gramps," Jan offered. "Eat slowly, as nerves choke you."

"Need time to think about the meeting today," he responded, as he pondered it for several minutes and then took a gulp and a forkful of cake. Cy yearned for luxury in his life but, as the patriarch of the family, felt obligated to set a higher standard.

"Only two for me today, Jan. Think I'm getting fat,"

joked Mark, patting his stomach. "And I get absurd in front of preachers." He'd actually not been to church in years, but he prayed and read his Bible daily. The crowds are what he avoided.

"And I'll take two and a half, Mom," Will added, mixing his juice with his milk. "I'm only part hungry. Nerves are better than usual," he jested. "If my gut gets too large, it'll hang over the stage and bang fans in the skull, causing fracases," he grumbled. Once the food was on the table, he merely picked at it.

"That's right, Will. Being unkempt can make a failure out of anyone," Jan said. "I know you're considering me, since I eat last." If they were alone, he wolfed the last one. Some of the time, Will's ego urged him to horde things. He was bright but beastly.

Will grinned at her and grumbled, "I know, Mom, that I'm always hungry and bolt it down, so I'll eat last. Dad and Gramps would like that, too." Will sampled them and added, "lacking a little cinnamon, but okay. Under the table as usual is Coon, hoping some will drop." Glancing down, he said, "there he is, right at Gramps' feet, leering with his tongue tip out." He shoved him away from the chair and wagged his finger to chastise the dog.

"Hope it doesn't send him after squirrels again," Cy cracked. "He knows they like acorns and thinks that those are in the pancakes. So he wants their acorns. A true fool. He'll get room isolation if he does it again, as none of us are risking rabies. Once he learns, it'll only take once."

Down the chimney a bird dived and fluttered into the kitchen, perching on the curtain over the stove. Coon growled, snapped and leapt at the stove to scare it away. But instead, it flitted onto his head. As he raced in circles to shake it off, it pecked his ear. Then Will heard the meow of the neighbor's cat at the door. "Only one way to get it out of here. Let Clancy in." So he opened the door; the cat sped in and onto the stove. Out flew the bird, but so did Coon, since Clancy won their last scrap.

"That took care of the bird and guess the dog's out for a while, too," Mark said.

"At least he'll get his play in," Jan said. "So he won't get bored with us away. Glad he can't climb the trees to catch the birds or squirrels. If he does, it'll be the last time he chases. Your job, Gramps, is to assure that the dog avoids other animals. If he runs amok, we have to give him away," Jan snapped with a clenched jaw.

"We won't get into that missy. If he goes, I go. It's unlikely that I'll be back, either. So if you don't want Will as an enemy, better think about that. We'll discuss it later, alone, if there's a problem," he growled. "Now Coon mainly darts at them and barks until he's hoarse. If a squirrel springs at him, he tumbles ten feet and mutes. After that, he's immobile and trembles. Yes sir, he really threatens those critters." For days, though, they dwelled on the squirrel biting Coon and knew that life would be mundane for him. If he approached other squirrels, he only whimpered at them. The topic of conversation shifted back to current affairs, seeing the pastor.

"Don't squawk about the travails of the dog to Jaba. He's not a vet and has no pets of his own. It'll agitate him so he may not assist you at all. Keep cool," Jan warned. Being perturbed at the whole affair, she was losing patience.

CHAPTER 28

Ignoring Jan, Mark said, "Hope you humor the office today. It'll ease my mind and make me almost enjoy the meeting. Of course, you've said the Pastor's like a best friend. I'll imagine I'm talking to you, Dad." Into a daze Mark slid, as his angst over the money grew.

"Good way to handle it," agreed Cy. "It'll benefit all of us. He's like therapy—puts most at ease but has been a control freak in the past, so hope we're not victims."

"I'm glad you're making it easier on yourselves," Jan added. "Don't let him advise without questioning. Be sure he's sincere."

"What have you got going today, Jan?" Mark asked. "Still working to lift those ladies into success? Meeting a few of them, I was shocked how well they fared in life." He saw them from rich and poor parents. "Wish you'd work into promoting yourself for a director of a more powerful agency. We could use the income if we don't get that money." He smirked, then flashed a toothy grin as he pointed above.

"When I feel like it, I will. Don't shove me into a foreign land without the training. I'll have it soon," she snapped. "This is a beautiful program, Mark," Jan said. "We have agencies and churches work together. For many recent programs it's an example."

To have Jan start the same program where they lived, foreign country dignitaries were sending representatives. From Japan Mr. Shimoto brought kimonos and four-hundred-pound sumo wrestlers to entertain them. Looking like huge bouncing beach balls, they hurled the girls onto their shoulders and paraded them around. A woman from the Philippines came with a water buffalo. It snorted and toppled desks, then shattered the wall to escape. From Africa a tribesman brought a giraffe that lapped its two-foot tongue into the refrigerator to swallow all of the snacks and then knocked itself out as it stalked into the doorway too short to get through. A tow truck had to winch him out.

"No matter how you look at it," Cy added, "everyone needs someone's hand to guide or support them. None of us are tough enough forever. But as we reach out to others to give what we are given, it reflects to us in the long run."

"If someone helps me, I return the favor to them or another," Will beamed. When he failed to get thanks, he went on.

"Let's all keep this in mind as we head out today, and in our tunnels will be light," Mark felt. "Dad, let's head for the man and Jan, grace. Will, look forward to your performance next week and Mrs. Smith. If she knocks you from the role, I'll have a chat with her. No one breaks a bond with you and I tolerate it. If we don't work it out, the principal's next. Stay strong!"

"And Dad, you and Gramps succeed with Jaba," Will boosted. If not, they would analyze the situation themselves.

"We love those ladies," Jan sighed. "It makes us flutter when any of them get ahead even a tad. They sweat, and it shows. Many husbands have returned to them, attended college or entered the military to elevate themselves in the world and make the house a home. When an attitude conflicts with our goals, we expel the one with it for three months. For her to return, she must accept probation for a month; if she fails, she's out for good. She reaped what she sowed. Her tares strangled her wheat."

Jan thought of her cubicle for one person, but it was a haven of near miracles wrought in women's lives. From any other program they had little hope, but through the Spirit, Mind, Body and Soul success, some of them had graduated from college and become teachers, social workers and other professionals. A few even became doctors and lawyers. One went to Nashville and was a country music star, and another was in Hollywood, on her way to the top starring in roles in some of the current blockbuster movies. Some began their own businesses, and they hired others who had completed Jan's program. It was a circle where success bred success, people learned to discard negatives in the trash and pick themselves up by their own souls, where God would do the rest of the job.

"That's as good as it gets for them," Cy said. "Maybe the rest of the world will sit up and take notice, too. If they don't, it's their loss, not your problem."

"You and Mark let me know how it goes with your world. I sense its benefit for both of you," Jan said. "But think for yourself as well."

"Not only do we think for ourselves, but we'll act it. We're getting advice not because we need it but to feel better about what we do." Cy said. He tapped his index finger to his head and flicked it toward her in defiance. "Mark and I are razors. We'll do the slashing," he growled, baring his teeth.

"Okay, pop. Don't cower when your plan collapses," Jan snorted and turned aside.

"Here's the bus. Bye everyone," Will said. "I'll be back after rehearsal today. Shannon's dad will drop me off." Glad I'm out of here, he thought.

"See you then," they said in unison.

When Will whisked out the door, he eyed the silver panel truck screech by. "There's the boy, green hair and backpack with his name on it," Bhagran barked. He hesitated to steal another moment's scrutiny with his binoculars. "Now, clip loaded, safety off, silencer on. Let's go babe." Fire in his eyes and a hint of anxiety evidenced by hand tremor, he shifted with his right hand, floored the chrome van to Will's driveway and cracked the window only enough to allow him a clear path for the barrel. Sunglasses and a fedora hid his features, spiked hair and protuberant, almost fluorescent, green eyes. "Three, two, one," was his countdown. "Fire one through five." The dirt in the yard flew up in response. "Clip two, five through ten," he boomed as the line of bullets cut a perfect swath around Will's prostrate body.

Something told Will to hit the ground as a total of fifty shots from Bhagran's automatic weapon made the trough around his body. Bhagran squealed off, Will sprang up, dusted himself off and dashed for the bus. He'd keep quiet about the incident, as he thought next time they wouldn't miss. But he'd really watch his back from now on. Bhagran had forgotten about the satellite cell phone Angus had sequestered in a clandestine compartment of the van. Ivanik was given one by the hotel clerk in the Marshalls and told to keep it. Angus had still pinned Bhagran's fate on him. He had the last laugh. It had a signal attuned to squeal if gunfire erupted through the van's cell phone speaker.

Ivanik eyed the phone as its screech halted him on the beach. He flicked it to his ear. "Yeah, who's interrupting my life?" he snapped into the speaker as he heard the engine rumble and Bhagran guffaw. The secret compartment of the van popped open as Ivanik's query was mid-stream. Bhagran snatched his phone and responded. "Lucky you there. This nine millimeter shows no favorites," he threatened, flipped the phone closed, then dropped it to the floor while waving the gun with one hand. His van had zig-zagged out of his other hand onto Interstate 85.

"Take care," Mark said to Jan. "We'll let you know what we find," and then he and Cy walked to the truck. They got in and heard Jan call to them.

"Bye," Jan said, "love both of you and will leave a message if my schedule changes." She snatched her briefcase, locked the door, plopped in her car and drove out behind them to her job. On the road the silver panel truck pulled aside her and remained for several minutes. Jan glanced at it, punched the gas and sped past him. "Looks like he knows where I go, too. Time to think about arming ourselves," she grunted. The truck edged to her left side and a double-barreled shotgun shot slipped out of the inch opening in the passenger window. The finger at the trigger pulled and buckshot scattered over her roof. She squealed over to the right onto the interstate and managed to lose the truck. "If we get the money, perhaps we better head to some island with plenty of sharks around it," she mumbled to herself. Sweat coursed down her forehead onto her collar as she sighed in relief and drove on.

Two men, Cy and Mark, were about to enter into the world of the church. Cy was a regular at the Rainbow Church of Our Lord. Mark wasn't. So he felt uneasy about asking a man of God to help them out of a very earthly dilemma. If they failed to find the owner of the money, maybe they could keep it. But Mark had his doubts and only saw trouble if they failed to do the right thing. Mark and Cy were silent driving to Pastor Jaba's office. Finally, they arrived at the church and turned into the lot facing the building. On the building was "Rainbow Church of Our Lord." Exiting the truck, they shuffled through the main door to the office.

"Hello, Mr. Cy," Amy Bailey, the secretary, chirped. "Go in. He's waiting for you. Thanks for having the faith to trust in his counsel." She was typing the Sunday service bulletin, and her waif body and pony-tailed auburn hair were covered by a red woolen shawl.

"Thanks. You've already reduced our concern," Cy said. He and Mark walked into the pastor's office and saw him with his Bible open, studying.

Ivanik's voice popped into the cell phone that Bhagran had absentmindedly left on once he had just left Greentown for Hartsfield. "Bhagran, you skunk. Pay for the job was rendered. Your cash is there for the doubloon exchange." Sure enough, Bhagran glanced back to see a black sack with hundred dollar bills flopping out the top. "Do it. Put a stint in the boy's family's curiosity and hit that church or I'll find you to finish it," he warned. So Bhagran turned about and headed toward the church.

For a week, Bhagran had bided his time by flipping cable channels, driving to a nearby park to jog and studying the stars with binoculars. Then the day came that the old man and young man sputtered along in front of him and crept into the church parking lot. "Rainbow Church of Our Lord. What kind of place would name itself that?" He wagged his head and chuckled. About a half mile before reaching the lot, he slid to the shoulder and cut the motor. "No matter. No church ever did a thing to help me. Let's cook this one," he growled as he fished for and found a box of matches in his pocket.

Breeching his thoughts, he gazed at the spire, turned the key and rumbled to the lot a minute after the two men entered the church doors. He parked nose out for a rapid escape. Then he sprang the door open, teetered as his seven-foot frame traversed the van's steps and strode in two seconds to the door. His left hand snatched the door open while his right hand clutched the matches. With his disguise still on, he mumbled to Amy, "Could you good people help a body in need?" Atop one another his hands lay as his arms formed an "x" across his chest, the matches still enclosed in his right palm.

"Sir," Amy responded, "Pastor handles all that. Shortly, he'll be with you, as soon as he's done with his meeting. Please, have a seat," she motioned toward the couch across from her.

"Sure, thanks." Bhagran sat only long enough to eye Amy's head return to the computer screen. Then he hopped to the trash can, struck a match and flicked it into a full load of paper. "Sorry, this will be painless," Bhagran grunted as he then uncoiled a ring of rope from his vest pocket. "One word, you die," he warned her. She gasped, then flung her hands to her lips before nearly fainting. He sealed her mouth shut with duct tape that he found on her desk and roped her hands behind her back, yanking the twist and knot until her hands flushed purple.

Terror gripped her as Bhagran leaped one step and was

out the door. To the van he hustled, cranked it up and spun out, then west to Hartsfield International Airport and after to Bombay. From there, he'd trek to Nepal, the Himalayas, Mount Everest and his last challenge, K2, the mountain that had lured hundreds and left fifty bodies frozen in its innumerable crevasses or on its unforgiving faces. Molokai, Hawaii was there for him when he retired.

Mark had to use the restroom, which was in the office, and saw the fire. "I've got to get this out," he barked. Amy was bug-eyed and trembled. Grabbing a nearby fire extinguisher, Mark snuffed the fire, then cut her loose. She explained the incident. He walked down the hall to catch Cy just as he was walking into Jaba's office. Scowling at Cy, he said, "We've got problems here now. I'll tell you with Jaba." They took seats.

"Hello Pastor," Cy hesitated. "This is a grave matter." He twisted his two head hairs.

"It had us on edge," Mark said. "So we realized it was critical to have more sound advice."

Jaba was a stocky man but had massive hands and eyes as black as his hair. His gray cashmere jacket was one of the few luxuries he allowed himself. As he grinned, any anxieties the two men had vanished and they sighed.

CHAPTER 29

Angus and Ivanik had left a decoy behind. Bhagran Amador was banished from India for numerous money laundering crimes that he was exonerated from in the courts but for which the banks believed he committed. At least a dozen thugs hired to assassinate him were at his heels constantly until he boarded the merchant ship to the U.S., which he stowed away on.

At seven feet tall, Bhagran had arms rippled with sinews, and was an accepted candidate for the National Basketball Association. With the other opportunities that tempted him, he opted for what he thought was a more rapid opportunity to gain wealth. His English was exceptional, and his visa had been granted rapidly. He was a marksman with a sniper's heart. As he contemplated his final duties in the U.S., he conversed with himself mostly, except for his brief tenure in Greentown to threaten two men, two boys and two women.

CHAPTER 30

"That's quite important, Mark. I've been to help out in events in other lands that allow me to see how good the U.S. has it. Compared to many areas, it's too easy here," Pastor Jaba said. "At times like these people oddly have less desire to help others. And that is so sad." He glanced at his spit-shined cordovan loafers and then peered out into the peach orchards of the farm next door. Their branches swayed, and he heard the whistling of the north wind through them. He cracked his knuckles and swiveled a foot to the left with a grinding creak that signaled a chair long overdue for replacement.

"There is a concern with our own problems, and it makes anything else pale beside it," Cy said. "I'm not so sure that having fewer problems makes it easy to look out for others in need, though."

"True, which is why church leaders can be overcome with loads that others won't handle," Pastor said. "We're the last link of help but the most important. It's never been just a Sunday job but mostly seven days a week." His calendar was full of notes and doodling of crosses, hymns, and jokes he created to entertain his members.

"Good thing you have strong arms to carry you," Cy said, pointing above. "So many times I've been hefted when life was more than I could bear. Few but you know what it's like when that happens."

"Now, before we get too far off track," Pastor said, "how about telling me what's going on with that money sack?" He drummed his fingers on his desk.

"First, I have to say that you're at risk here, too, Pastor. Amy had a seven-foot guy walk in behind us to burn her up in the office. Likely the guy who dropped the money," said Mark. He flicked his ear hair several times.

"Obviously, he's knows where we are, and he's getting closer. We'll have to expect anything anywhere. From now on we all keep our eyes roving," Cy said.

"Sure," Mark said. "If we want to stay alive, that's what we'll do." Every few minutes he arose and glanced out the window for any more intruders.

"Well, when I was at a doctor's new house working inside, a step-van with shiny sides flipped off some missing wood of ours, and a huge sack of money slid out the back of it and underneath it. Then it drove off," Cy said.

"Did you see the driver?" Pastor asked. He glared at Cy and stroked his coal-black curly hair.

"Not a bit. Windows were dark and he drove out fast," Cy said. "The tag was blacked out too, with a cover on it."

"Did you call the doctor to ask him about it yet? Or you think he could be in on some wrong activity?" Pastor asked. He eyed them nervously as he said this.

"We let no one except family know about it yet," Mark

said. "With us still innocent, it's too risky to tell a wrong person." He bowed his head for a moment.

"I tell you what," Pastor said. "I'll call the doctor from here and see how he reacts. Then we'll go from there." He glanced at Cy and Mark with sympathetic eyes.

"But don't mention us yet, to be sure it doesn't carry us up in it. Please," Cy begged.

"Sure, I'll only say that when you were there you saw the lumber pile and a big sack crushed under it. If it could be damaged by rain, maybe he should check on it. There will be no mention of you seeing money in it. But I'm a minister and can't lie to find out information. I'll simply tell him what you saw and hang up. Then you let me know what you find there today. Or in a while we can drive by to see any change," Pastor said.

"The last idea sounds best," Cy said. "If you come, then we can have a witness if there are problems. Thanks, Pastor." He smiled and twiddled his two hairs again.

Dialing Doctor McKenzie, Jaba merely got a curt response. He was told, "What, I've had some carpenters on that job but have no idea where a big sack came from. Nothing I ordered would be sent like that. If something's wrong, call the sheriff, please. My workers, Cy and Mark McGinn, don't need any lost sleep. You can call later to let me know a solution. I'm at the hospital until late but can call back. Thanks for letting me know about this." Then the doctor hung up.

With providential help, three men would find the solution to a vexing problem. You seldom heard about these things on the news but only in stories. Money didn't grow on trees. It originally came from the U.S. mint and had its home mostly in banks, store tills, but also in ladies' purses and men's wallets. It didn't blow in from the wind, and the only trucks that had ever lost it were armored cars on highways, occasionally. Until caught, some people would stop to retrieve the loose bills. For their honesty, those who returned their find often got minute rewards. But the McGinn family would truly be lucky or blessed, however you look at it.

"I don't know any more about the source of the money than before the call," Pastor said. "But the doctor says he has no clue what's going on. Looks like the people dumping the money had an address mix-up, and it happened to be his place. We'll see if the money is there before talking about it any more." His brows furrowed and then flickered.

"Okay by us," Mark said. "Shall we go? Would you like us to drive, Pastor?" The pastor thought about it for a moment but shook his head no.

"No, Mr. McGinn. I feel we need to be in a car no one has seen in the area. Mine has room for us all," Pastor said. "We can go now. Amy, take any calls, please. We should be at least a few hours," he said as he strode past Amy's desk.

"Yes, sir. Have a good morning, and I'll pray for you." She was still trembling.

The men walked out to the pastor's white Ford and got in, then turned out onto the main road for the long drive. Time went slowly, and to pass the hour they listened to church radio. "Take it easy, gentlemen, as I'll do the trip, and you let me know when we get close to where we turn," Pastor said.

"Thanks, Pastor, for all that you're doing. We're grateful and hope that sack is gone so it's over," Cy groaned. Driving on, they finally arrived at the house. When they looked in the driveway, the sack with cash was gone but in its place was a smaller one. As they pulled into the driveway, the pastor rolled the window down and unraveled the bag's ribbon.

"Looks like some kind of gold coins," Pastor observed. "This is as strange as before. For some reason, this could be an exchange for the cash. It could be less but maybe not. If it's pure gold, there may be over a million dollars, but we won't count on it. Cy, you and Mark can keep on this job, but I'd want this bag out of here first. It's up to you." Then the silver panel truck rattled by and splayed .45 bullets along the ground in front of them. They all slammed their heads to the seats and lay there several minutes.

"You're right," Cy said with a scarlet face, perspiring heavily. "For a few days we'll put this on hold and work in town. The doctor will okay it, and we'll say that we had critical business, but be back shortly. Thanks so much," Cy said, pumping the pastor's hand until it nearly snapped his neck. Scanning the road for more trouble, Mark and the pastor trembled and rotated their heads.

They drove back to the church office and strode inside to rap. "Don't let this concern you, Cy," Pastor advised. "It will work out so you and Mark can get back to the job. But for a few days, don't blame you for working elsewhere. Those bullets were rather convincing. If you need me, call or drop by, please. I'll tell Amy to give me the message right away, if I'm out." He slid notes about on his computer.

"Thank you, Pastor. Will do. Look forward to working here whenever you need me, also. Take care," Cy said. He and Mark took turns hugging him, then hopped to the truck and sped to their next job. The truck thumped a bit, and they knew the bald spot on the rear tire was enlarging.

Bhagran was given the McGinns' address, and he had kept a distant vigil with binoculars to note where Will lived. He said to himself, "There's the boy again. Green hair and backpack with his name on it." Shannon's dad had dropped Will and Shannon off, and the two boys rousted in the front yard when the silver van drove up. Bhagran, masked, jumped out, slapped them, then tied them up. He gave them a warning. "Keep quiet, and you'll be okay. Somebody knows about that money, and I'm not the one who found it. In the jungle of Brazil a friend dug it up and gave it to me. We don't know who buried it, but a note in the chest said it was three hundred years ago. Quit getting nervy on me," he growled at his quarry when he saw their legs shaking.

"When Gramps gets hold of you, he'll snap you," Will threatened. "He could be back anytime."

"Time for the duct tape. You're too noisy." The man taped their mouths and shoved them onto their backs. As they struggled, he continued to talk. "Now to live well for life as did my friend, I took some of the money and am dumping the rest anywhere I can. Sorry your grandpa and dad got involved. I have to keep them scared so they don't get too snoopy. Soon I'm heading for my island. You'll likely be given the money, Will, my boy, and can treat your friends for years. When they have it rough, give 'em a thousand or two and tell 'em spend it wisely. Maybe more later."

A few blocks away a car skirted a curb, and the man leapt in the van, squealing off. The car turned away, and the driver failed to see them. After a half hour, Shannon slipped his arms loose, then finally untied his legs and jerked his duct tape off. He cut the ropes off Will with his Swiss Army Knife, and Will ripped his tape off.

"Imagine that, Will, you might be rich," Shannon said. "I'll only ask for help when I really need it. Won't tell anyone about this if you don't."

"No chance. It might jinx our family getting the money,

Shannon. I'll help you and Sally Lu even when you don't need it. If I'm rich or poor, you're my friends."

"Thanks, Will. I'll head home now. My stomach's gone, and I'm taking some antacids." He galloped three houses up to his yellow rancher and scrambled in the door.

"Sure, see you after we get this mess figured out," and Will went in to rehearse.

In the future the silver van and its driver could well add problems to the McGinns' lives. They would adapt the best they could and were tough to beat. The incidents were affecting friends, family and a church leader. So it was critical to unravel the mystery and terminate the terror being wreaked upon those involved. Work and prayer were needed.

CHAPTER 31

"What do you think if we go to the McGinn Scottish museum site, son," Cy said, "so the mayor can get out the word that in a year it should be open? Now is a good time, since next summer is that big culture day week-long event," Cy said. What Will and Shannon had been through they failed to know and weren't likely to find out.

"Oh wonderful, Dad. I knew we discussed it but didn't know when it would bear fruit. That will be the most satisfying work to date, and fortunately the state and Scottish government are both giving the money to provide for it in Greentown," Mark said.

Bhagran had driven to the nearest hotel, the Danesworth, checked in and was up by 4 a.m. to course Will's home area. After several days, he had noted an old man and one about forty backing from a driveway. Parked at the end of the street, barely out of sight, Bhagran scanned and saw them travel the opposite direction. Gunning the engine, he slammed gears and followed a half mile behind. After three miles, he stopped as they entered a field with a commercial building jutting from the earth surrounded by some scraggly pines.

Entering the five-acre area, Mark and Cy viewed several tall pines and cedars as well as wavering grassland that had been there for centuries. The museum would be in the center of the area, and few trees would be cut down. From the road it would still be visible, and people from all over would learn how at least one country in Europe lived. The shortbread cookies were a treat that kids and adults both would like.

"Now, I have plans in here, son, sealed in a waterproof tube so that they'll be good until the museum is done," Cy said. He hefted an aluminum container. "On this one we'll labor more since it's a bit more than a big house. But a lot more love we'll put into it while working on it." Bhagran had tailed Cy and Mark to the museum. With stealth, he had continued to the field, hurtled over the curbing past the truck, then circled it as he rolled his window down, then opened fire on the men before they could exit. As Cy spoke, the silver van swooshed by, ran up into the grass and missed running into their truck by a foot. Then a .45 pistol slipped out of a partially open window, and they were fired upon again, this time nicking Mark on his right ear lobe. To stop the bleeding, he pressed a rag to his ear. They tumbled out and dashed into the trees to hide while the van screeched off, out of sight. "Son, he knows we've seen the money now, and we're really going to have to watch our backs. We'll handle the risk, though. The Scottish do." In relief, Mark groaned.

When Bhagran bound back onto the road, he whipped to the curb at the nearest intersection, wheeled left and smoked tires as he entered the main road. "That was a challenge. Could've returned fire," he mused while driving back to the hotel. Sweat coursed his neck and lodged in the velour cover of the seat, its scarlet color fading to a hue of olive green. "Penney dye," he snorted. "A half-billionaire and his buddy gifted with millions buy Chinese felt for my comfort. No problem. One more dirtball to sweep, then I'm off." Reaching the hotel, he spun into the lot and screeched to park, then wrung his hands in anticipation.

Every few minutes Mark squirmed, as he imagined a bullet in his brain next time. Cy cranked his neck behind to watch for a return and spat constantly in anxiety. Finally, Mark could speak again. "This will be a critical work," he said. "Even if they're not Scottish, many people see museums as being part of family pride."

"Oh, but there are a few Scottish here who will be part of the program anytime. If they could avoid being teased, they'd wear their kilts now. Driving by their houses, I've heard those old bagpipes blowing my favorite tunes. A few times I've shed some tears and sang with them, then gone home to gaze at the big pictorials of the homeland. After that, I've longed for the castles, green grass, moors and cows mooing with contentment on the hillsides."

"What about the sheep, Dad? Don't they make wool clothing there, too?"

"Why yes, son, how could I forget? In my cedar chest are the softest sweaters."

"Forget clothing. It's the water monster legend that I'm interested in." Mark's eyes bulged.

CHAPTER 32

They thought of Nessie, or the Loch Ness monster. Many had seen a dragon-like creature with a long body that had fins and wings on it. It roamed Loch Ness lake and terrorized those who had seen it. From thirty to fifty feet long was its length. This meant that it could easily sink large boats or even some ships that would come through the waters there. Now there was talk of dragons, knights who slew them and people who perished by their fire-breathing mouths. Picture this: On a boat with fifty adults and children is a party. Big balloons, cake with candles, and all kinds of presents lay on the seats of the boat. Then along comes Nessie, circling the boat, surfacing and spitting water and fire around them. Some of the adults jump overboard and are swallowed up by her. Coming closer to screaming children is the creature.

Away swims the monster, and all think it is gone. But it returns with its babies, overpowering the thirty-foot boat.

When the boat throttles its motor full speed, Nessie and her brood swiftly tail them as they circle, trying to evade the slashing of the dragon-snake's tail onto their helpless flesh. Across the lake is a fisherman who races to it with a harpoon and rifle to save the foundering boat. Thrusting a spear at the creature, he sees it turn on him with its teeth bared and sinuous body undulating to destroy him.

As the people in the boat glare at the scene, he lifts his rifle. They know if he misses that they are the next bait for it. Water roils and splashes the boat masses, and the fisherman takes aim. He fires, only striking the tail, and the creature returns with a vengeance but now wavers between trying to attack him and the boat with women, men and children in it. He has an idea and tells them, "At the same time both of us will squeeze it, then I'll get a good aim and either kill it or drive it back under the water."

The other boat heeds his directive and gets so close that the passengers see its pupils, narrow and cat-like, but its eyes are as grey-black with death as a shark's. It has elliptical scales that wave in and out, to and from its body like gills. In the sun they shimmer a golden brown. Like fiery coals, its eyes glow and glare at all around it who wish to destroy it. The fisherman takes another bead on Nessie, this time firing to strike her in the head, drilling a hole that doesn't bleed but sends it into contortions, away and under the water with all of its young.

As the boat with passengers narrows on the fisherman, all jump the gunwale to hug, kiss and thank him for his help. This was none other than Cyrus McGinn before he sailed to the U.S. and left his beloved homeland for the love of his mail correspondent, Maggie McConnahugh. Becoming a hero in Scotland, he had to answer inquiries about Nessie for months. To maintain his sanity, he escaped, and Maggie became his reason for doing so. They fell in love and married. Cy's mind returned to the present, and he and Mark faced their daily concerns. Other than having a sack of cash, they were simple home builders.

"Will could learn some Scottish hymns, give them a show and get good training before an audience," Cy said.

"Mrs. Smith would be impressed with his learning foreign songs," Mark said.

"The whole school would learn about the Scottish and relate to all peoples worldwide."

"Live skits entertain and explain," Mark said.

"Let's have an exchange program to send young people there, and theirs will come here for a time." Cy knew it would work.

"When I was in school, Dad, we had a Scottish student. He couldn't imagine so many cars on our roads. They have fewer cars and far more buses, trains and tram cars. Ian McConnell was seventeen. Once he returned to Scotland, in a year he would graduate. He loved the people here the most, since a hug or handshake was always in order. The Scots were rather cool, Ian said. But he still loved his land and missed his family."

"How did the fellow your school sent there say he fared?" Cy asked.

"She was a young lady, actually, and successful. For months students wrote letters asking her back. Parents offered to pay her way there during a school holiday. Her name was Jill O'Neill, and she was bright, speaking three languages. Later, she had a Scottish boyfriend," Mark said. "But in Northern Ireland she was in conflict and never returned to the U.S. From her parents we heard that she died in a bombing there."

"That's a shame, and I'm sure it gave everyone heartache. When we invite someone here, it's hoped they aren't shot by our wild man in a van," Cy said. "Now, luckily, the foundation has been poured, and all the storage units filled with what we need for the project. The sun is out, and we'll get the frame up today. Positive thinking, some sweat and a few tools will do it."

CHAPTER 33

"Okay, Dad. Let's go and have at it," Mark said. Exiting the truck, they picked up tools and went to work. In four hours, they finished eight hours of building.

"After the display area is done, we'll do the stage areas for the performances. Pew seats will encourage visitors to sit closer together and bring in more families."

"Skylights will let sun in so it feels more like outdoors, and cloudy days will be better," Mark added.

"For the little ones we'll have a play room. That's what's missing from most places for adults. If you make a place for all ages, more will come."

They looked out and saw a storm brewing. When they thought about it, there was never a tornado in the area, so they eyed the sky and talked. Drawing nearer for an experience to remember or forget, the mind's choice, it was what Cy and Mark wanted to forget, as they had another lingering concern.

"We'll keep Will out of there, Dad. You know how he is about that, keeping small kids entertained. If he becomes a singer, he'll have plenty of fans, since he can relate so well."

"If we put a sign up saying, 'for kids only,' he'd figure it out, son. That's the way to put up a keep out sign."

"Dad, he'll be too busy with choir to come by. Even in summer, plays keep them fresh and their minds working. Creating is constant and a good thing. No one wants a world void of new ideas."

"For the museum, entrance will be round, center a rectangle and corners are pyramids. No matter the direction it's seen from, it'll draw eyes." Cy and Mark noticed something wicked. On the far horizon, a dark wall cloud formed. Ominously, it swirled toward them at twenty miles per hour. A funnel dropped out of it, and Cy said, "Hit the ditch," where they cowered as the freight-train noise from the twister almost deafened them. "Look at it pick up cars and hurtle them a hundred yards away." The house across from them was next. Down the street, Cy saw it thrash the Caffeine Cafe, his favorite haunt, to pieces. "Time to say a prayer, now, Mark. Get to work." They both bent their heads to their chests and asked to have the rest of Greentown spared from the storm's wrath. In a few moments, the wind disappeared, the cloud raced toward the east, and the sun shone again. A few had been injured, none killed, they heard later that day.

"It's another miracle, Dad. We didn't do it. But we asked for protection and got it. It doesn't happen every time but did this one. So we can show we're thankful, let's smile and beam those up. It shouldn't happen again, as it never has before. That was a test of faith, and we passed. Our future depends on keeping that belief. Thanks, Sir." Mark paused, glanced at the sky again, then said, "The museum photos for the postcards will make most visitors look at it."

"When they gaze at it, they'll want to come inside. A few dollars entry is what we'll charge," said Cy. To many, that's not much, so they chose it.

"That will make it more attractive. Asking for donations will get visitors in, almost like magic."

"Working on this, we're away from Doc's house. He's a good guy, but we'll avoid being part of where that money came from. If we found it in another way, that's different. Like a pirate chest of doubloons washed up on the beach or finding a huge gold nugget in the mountains. It's safer and would really be ours."

"Yeah, Dad, it could happen if we traveled much, but not in this area. We had it dumped in a strange driveway." He still envisioned rummaging for dollars.

"And for a while now we ignore it. We'll let it work itself out. From one with wisdom, it's the best idea. Pastor Jaba had the calling for a reason, to help others. He can work out his own problems, so with his spare mind he gives. Outside the church world that's less common, though."

"That's why it's a calling. To handle that for years, help from above is needed. None of them do it on their own," Mark said.

Working with people who had numerous problems, such as divorce, diseases, job conflicts, Pastor Jaba had even been into war zones. It seemed simple to solve a problem with a money find. Turn it into authorities and let them deal with it. But if this were millions of dollars, he, Mark or Cy may be blamed for taking it. That could mean jail time, and Cy didn't want that again. Jaba knew to find out who it belonged to. So with dogged determination he would work.

"No one would try it alone. Only when the Big Guy

is in on it. He sees the whole picture that we can't start to draw. Then, He can start and finish it how he wants to. We pray that we stay in the plan as long as possible," Cy said.

"To do that, we're good to others constantly, not only when we feel like it. Part-time love won't work. For God nor the world."

"Few things makes me feel worse than being friendly, then lashing out. I can't do both, even if I try. It's not in me. At times most people get angry, and some may be mostly happy. Anger can help rarely but only if it's controlled."

"I'm glad that my teacher was you, Dad. It's not in me either. Will and Jan have argued and then talked it out. For others, staying bitter can make a hard life."

"We have it better than most, harder than some, but if we think it's good, times will often get easier. That's the way it goes."

"And the only way to handle life."

"It's the way we want to look at our own lives."

"Reading the Bible daily is how to figure out what to do and when."

The McGinns needed to make more time to do that. Cy read his daily, but the rest of the family might neglect it for days at a time. Although there was a void, they didn't realize why. There were five Bibles in the house, all in plain sight. So it was the thought of them that would get them to read. Cy set the example.

CHAPTER 34

"Speaking of handling life, this building represents a big chunk of all our lives," said Cy. "The whole family has a stake in our history."

"Yes, Dad, the museum is about the past and where your father and mother came from."

"Many have forgotten their roots. With theirs, African-Americans had so much pain, can't blame them. Same with Native Americans. But with Europeans, Asians, and Middle Easterners, there should be a stronger desire to connect to their old world."

"Knowing the past prevents future mistakes. It's your family's future that a poor past can affect. If you attack the poor past, it's less likely to hurt you." He knew what he did could affect him later.

"Yes, son, everyone should know their family tree. It can benefit health, mind and education when family's aware of them."

Most are unaware of their family history. Grandmothers make pies, cakes, milk shakes and other good things to eat. They'll tell you about the past and long for better days. Then they ask about school, how it's going and where are you going in life. Sometimes they talk about Grandpa, Mom, Dad or their pet dog or cat. When Mom or Dad won't listen and sometimes don't help problems, they support you. Living near them can be all the better. See and talk to them often, as Will did.

Cy might go fishing, camping or take Will to the stores and buy things for him. To be tough, he may say to go out and win that game but play hard regardless. He was like gold. In the yard, or on the old Packard he liked to work. If something was broken, there he was to repair it pronto. Will remembered the time he first yanked his false teeth out and chased after him with them. If he had a good job or a hard, dirty one, he took it as it came. He said that if Will stuck with something and never thought about failing, maybe he could be a pro baseball player, football player, actor or singer on a big record label. Cy told Will to listen; he didn't live to be old by being dumb. He knew how to survive and thrive. If Will didn't succeed, it wasn't his fault. Instead of listening to him, maybe he talked. It's wisdom they have, and only living and life teach it, not school or books. Grandparents can both help you be a winner if you want to be. It's up to you.

"When we start giving value to our older people, we'll be much happier. They are a wondrous museum of how to love life as long as you can and pass that feeling to others," said Mark. "It's best if they teach us as long as possible. Talking to them often can allow that."

"Yes, we're museums of the spirit. The spirit of strength, courage, wisdom and honesty. Over the years those have declined. We need to work with the young, like Will, to bring it all back."

"It's what made the country so great and gave us respect from the world for so long. We must know who we are putting our trust in. For example, teachers, company bosses, those in Congress and the White House."

"A vote is not all there is, but it's the soul behind the face. That's what will be the right or wrong, good or bad for us."

"We search ourselves before we consider who will run the land, and knowing ourselves takes work, prayer, staying close to our families and being honest with them and our friends," Mark said. "Truth helps us know ourselves."

"That provides the greatest strength of all. In all the other traits of people with few problems is honesty. Feeling good about what you say and do makes the soul follow naturally."

Little about honesty and honor is taught in schools. Will is lucky to learn about it from at least one teacher. Mrs. Smith not only teaches music but how it can benefit others with Will's talent. From Will and all of her students she expects the best. Will practices daily and knows his future success depends upon it. He thinks not of receiving but how he can return what he's taught. For him to reach his goals it may take years, and he knows that. So he takes life day by day.

"If you could, as the saying goes, read a person like a book to know if they were honest, life would be sweeter. In the world much pain is due to a lack of honesty and thus, honor," Mark said.

"There would be far fewer billionaires and multi-millionaires if honor came first. Those who hope to achieve success must be honest at some time but some are not all of the time."

Honest is what most want to be, and it can really pay off. If you have your own company, honesty makes you. Working for others means that they want you to excel at your job. If someone else takes something, the boss should know. In all you do honesty breeds success. Being dishonest can lead to lost friends and family failing to trust you. If someone dropped a thousand dollars, you'd have to decide whether to keep it or give it back. Returning it may be difficult, and some people wouldn't, since that's a huge sum to many. But if you don't, money could become only a way to get ahead. If you don't earn it, you may look for the easy way, a way to lose in life and love. Work at it to be a winner.

"We'll be honest with the museum to succeed. Museums are honest, as few of them, probably none, give owners wealth," Mark said. He regretted starting the project.

"That's why we left the money sack where it was, and we're not rich now. We stay away from what's not ours. If we are awarded it because no one claims it, then we'll decide what we'll do with it and for others."

Wealth passed down in families can be good or bad for a young heir. Some learn to enjoy life, travel, large houses, Maserati or Lamborghini cars, land with horses and ocean-front views as well as friends. But others blow money so fast that they forget where it came from. Conrad Hilton, Rockefellers, Gettys are some who passed on wealth to younger ones. Most would love to inherit millions to make life easier, but few will. So we must work hard to make our own way in the world. If we achieve wealth, we are blessed and should use it for others as well as ourselves.

CHAPTER 35

"Let's head home shortly, as Jan and Will are expecting us," Cy said. "We've scoured the plans and have a month of supplies moved and ready to go, plus we've done four hours of hard work with the wall braces up. Tomorrow we can set the sheetrock for the masons to work around." Cy sensed there would be danger going home.

"Okay, Dad, I agree. I'll drive, and you guide. While you relax tonight, I'll review the list of folks who've worked with us as contractors to call."

Cy said, "Mainly, workers must believe in what we are creating." They drove toward home when the silver van appeared again. The driver fired on them, and this time shattered the passenger window and nicked Cy's neck so that a trickle of blood streamed onto his shirt collar. Cy fingered the wound and noted it was minor. "Mark, this is getting hazardous, and we better write these incidents down for evidence, if needed."

"Sure, I'll do that, and we'll mention it to Jan, too."

"Hey, here we are. Almost missed the driveway talking business," said Cy. "Hope Will is tops in that performance, as he sure labors to succeed."

"He'll do well because he believes in himself."

Will ran out to meet them, bounding, waving a paper and spouting of being the lead in the play. "Dad, the lead Mrs. Smith chose took the part in another major play. So I'll play Daddy Warbucks in "Little Orphan Annie." He felt it was the role of his life.

"Wonderful, son. You've worked hard and deserve it. But rehearsals will be a bit more involved now. I'm sure Sally Lu and Shannon understand if you miss some days of being out and about." He wished that he had more time with Will.

"Oh, they were in the auditorium when I got the part, since they're doing background singing," Will admitted. "So they often have to be in there with me. And they're learning lines for the next play that I may be in. We'll have a great time."

Cy worked with Will on his rehearsals to assure that he repeated every line perfectly. After all, it was a reflection on him if Will made a fool of himself. For listening in his sleep, Will recorded the lines. He wanted to win.

"When your friends support you like this, it's always a winner," said Cy. "We'll enjoy being at the practice, too. Hard work makes a polished performance."

"Getting it right is a treat to watch, as you enjoy the final work so much more. To repeat it so many times is difficult," Mark said.

"You get your lines right to keep other actors smooth," Will offered. "When you get it right, there's support. Hey

Gramps, where did your window go?" he asked, gawking at the open space. Cy was silent.

Jan glanced out and said, "Okay, unless everyone only wants to act like they ate dinner tonight, come in and wash up. It'll be ready in an hour. It's beans and sandwiches, but they're my special baked ones we all like."

"Okay," Mark said. "We wouldn't want to miss that favorite. And Dad, watch Coon, as he tries to hop on the chair when that's on the menu."

"Right, as soon as Jan put it on the table last time, he ate my sandwich. And looked so innocent when I asked if he got it," Cy said. "But I can't love him any less for it. He acts so sorry after it." Glancing at the dog, he flashed a grin and winked.

"I think Jan keeps the eye out for him now, though, so he's become a good boy," Mark said. "He only eyes them but keeps the peace."

"I'll feed him before Mom sets the table," Will said.

"That's the idea," agreed Jan. "During family meals a full tummy makes any pooch better. Works every time."

Will rummaged for the best food that Coon got a few times a week. He poured it in his silver dish and plenty of spring water in his water bowl. As the family sat down to their meal, Coon ate and drank, then straggled to Cy's bed to lay. Blinking his eyes, he pined for the days when he chased squirrels. As he struggled to sleep, a dream made him shudder and jerk, so that he remained awake for hours. Cy and Will came in to pet him, and he finally relaxed and closed his eyes.

"To be such a big dog, Coon has the mind of a pup. In his sleep he trembles, but when awake, he gives himself to us. Hope he's around much longer, as we'd miss him so much, it might make us mope a while. As long as we

love him as he loves us, many more years of companionship we'll provide each other. It'll mean working daily with
him," Will said. "We need to pray for him as we do for us."
Coon's ears wriggled in response.

CHAPTER 36

"Speaking of work," Cy said, "W has become top billing for the play. And we made a pretty good dent in the museum today. But we were almost run over by the silver van, and he shot my window out and nicked my neck with a bullet."

"If that keeps up, we may have to get the law involved," Jan said sternly. "I see that Mark was hit too. Please go clean it up and put antibiotic on it. Then later we'll discuss it." She was involved with Will now. "Should they worsen we'll see a doctor. For rehearsal schedule changes, I have Mrs. Smith's number. We've already talked, and she feels this is one of Will's best opportunities to begin acting. Will loves singing, and the play exposes him to the community. A Hollywood producer is scouting for a young actor to star in a movie next year. Greentown is one of his stops. That will add to the museum's value."

Mark stood, thrusting his hands in his pockets. For Mark this provoked contention. Jan decided that Will stayed in choir, but Mark wanted him strong. So they argued about the choices.

"To become a singer Will needs choir," Jan said. She gave Mark a threatening glare.

"You know that there's only a one percent chance of him making it in music? Let him become a karate expert, and he may start a chain of instruction studios," Mark snapped.

"What a foolish idea. He's moving along well in the arts, and he has to stay there," she said. She eyed Will and envisioned him performing at a big concert hall.

"I'll tell you what, if he stays in choir and doesn't make it in music, I'm moving out when he fails in the world." Mark inched away from Jan as he said this.

"Well, if he stays in karate and doesn't go to college, I'll be leaving. Okay, now that it's settled, we sleep in separate rooms for awhile." She turned away from Mark.

"Sure, I need a wife, not a warrior, so I'll sleep on the couch for a time," he said.

To totally reconcile, it took Jan and Mark six months, and they stayed together for Will. Though they put on a facade of love, the emotions were clamped for a while. The group got back to the conversation at hand.

"We'll have a local or national celebrity for the museum," Cy broke in.

"But I won't have time to sing or perform there, Dad, at least not for a while," Will said. "When I'm off I can." He detested being like a relic.

"Son, Dad and Gramps will run the museum. Only whenever you want to visit you can, right guys?" Jan asked.

"Of course," said Cy. "If he's a national star, we'll use hats and sunglasses to go out, as paparazzi or fans would find the house."

At the museum that night there were oddities. Spirits

of dead Scottishmen whom Cy used to know danced and played bagpipes. With hammers and nails they worked much of the building so that Cy and Mark could rest.

"Hope that money doesn't ruin 'em," one said. "It does much of the time. What do you think McHenry? You know so much about people. Look at this museum."

"Don't think it will. A preacher's involved," McHenry said. They all knew what most humans and spirits know: too much money can make people crazed.

"It happened to me. Had to start giving some away so I could think again," McTavish said.

"What say we waltz over to Doc's house, take the money to sea and toss it?" McInery added.

"Let's have 'em find out for themselves, if they live long enough. All of us were rich in our lives. Now we're nailin' things in the after," McDowell said.

"If they don't use it right, then we take it and melt it. As ingots, it'll be worth the most," McFlynn said. "Years will pass to find that out. It's settled then." They all got back to building, and it was quiet after.

Responding to Cy, Jan said, "Well, let's not rush him into that life, nor take the one he now has away. But he has a direction now, even if later he becomes a scientist or doctor."

Having goals is direction. From childhood to adult, a goal makes life point up. It's excellent to have friends to keep goals. Will relies on Sally and Shannon to pump him up, so every day he sings, it's a step nearer a new life as a song artist. In his mind, he's already there. So any kid who sees a goal gained is near it.

"If he gives something useful to the world, whether art, medicine, help to the poor, food for the soul, it's all well," Cy said. Will wished to donate his voice to others.

"I'm giving to others, since Mrs. Smith is a good example. When out, she leaves a note, 'take care of my special ones, please,'" Will said. "That's a rare teacher."

Few students like teachers since they remind them of parents. When one guides a student to success, the feeling is one of gratefulness. Will saw himself improve.

Emerson said, "Gold and jewelry are not gifts but apologies for gifts; the only true gift is a portion of thyself." During birthdays, Christmas and other holidays the McGinns spent much more time than money. They gave of themselves.

"Receiving when you've given back evens out," said Jan.

"By working now, Dad gives," said Mark. "More important than the money he makes is feeling useful. It's using our total talent to create."

"When you sing a song, act or do anything that others will enjoy," said Cy, "enjoy it for yourself first, then others will more likely have an interest in it."

"Cooking is something I want to do, although you won't stop enjoying good meals!" Jan chirped.

"All of us love Will singing at home, but he needs others to appreciate him," said Mark. "He'll share with others here and worldwide."

"In Greentown is where I start, though," said Will. "Going slower and being a kid will make my early years. You can't do them over."

CHAPTER 37

Will knew many child TV or movie stars never had a kid's life. Work and making money overwhelmed them, and there was little time to enjoy it. Until he was eighteen, he'd never accept a contract for singing.

While he is in school, Will travels to states and countries: Australia, Japan, Scotland, Africa, Egypt, China, New Zealand. This gives him places to sing and shows that he can adjust to touring later. He meets people who promote him and listened while Cy continued to extol the value of learning from mistakes.

"That's true," said Cy. "Starting over, some could right mistakes and others could enjoy life again. But we can only remember what we did. Then be glad it helped make us a better person later."

"What we all do best is to use knowledge to help others," Jan said. "Whether what happened is good or bad, we've gone through it to relate to others better."

"For years, I've avoided criticizing," said Mark. "I know that if I goofed, I'd want a break. At least to hear it said, 'no problem, we've been there.'"

"Occasionally a student criticizes another," Will said. "But I say to them that there's something to like about everyone, so compliment them next time."

"Hanging around Sally Lu, who has been a natural at keeping peace, may have helped, too," admitted Jan. Sally traveled the world with her wealthy uncle, so she knew about what makes people different and react differently. She never thought one way.

"I've heard her advise someone, and I think like her. Having her as a friend's been a blessing. People listen to her," said Will. "When her mom and dad squabble, she ends it."

"That's why they have one of the closest families in Greentown. It'll be a lucky guy who marries her some day," said Jan.

"Yep, he'll feel she's almost too perfect and will need to be peaceful himself," Cy said.

"We need Sally Lu's all over to teach peace," added Mark.

"She's not sure if she'll ever get married and may be a missionary or work with the poor overseas. Going into the military as a chaplain, she could maybe do both," Will offered. "I've met a few chaplains who came to visit school and think it's an interesting life."

"That's right," said Jan. "They serve others during peace and war. Chaplains are peaceful, serving all of the military and never entering battle. In other countries they deal with Americans." Chaplains, unlike ministers in peaceful areas, often serve in war zones that have the risks of the soldiers there. They may be injured when their base or area is attacked.

"The job may or may not be safer than that of a missionary," Cy said. "If they are in war zones, the enemy may not know they're ministers."

In the military is a different world. Only those in there know it. Some feel alone; others may fit in and grow to have friends who will be there for them years later. Like any job, there's good and bad. It's all in prayer, faith and being true to yourself.

"A chaplain tries to improve lives and works with families, people with problems and also leads churches on bases and posts," said Mark. "They leave most outside work to the private churches."

"We can assist others wherever we are. Our own family, neighbors, friends, so on," Cy said.

"If our own lives are going well, spread that cheer around. Everyone can use positive to brighten up their day. No matter the weather, let's make it better," said Jan.

"In school I treat others fairly," said Will. "In some way it returns and opens my heart."

"Sometimes I did that and still fought when I was a boy. But people knew that I strived for better, and it wore off on them," Cy said.

"People thank me for small things," Will said. He remembered his friend, Joe, an amputee whose books he carried.

News can be harsh. If it is ignored and the best of life focused upon, anguish can be reduced, and more rainbows can be seen. It's turning a deaf ear to it. Blot it out of the mind, and think about what is bliss.

"It's important that others treat us well," Cy said.

"Being congenial causes no pain. But harsh can cause

headaches, backaches, leg aches, you name it!" Mark said. In the past some of his coworkers unhappy about small things complained to others, who often shunned them.

"When I'm treated well, I'll pass it to others," said Will.

"In sermons all the time Pastor refers to the Golden Rule. 'Do unto others as you would have them do unto you.'" Cy knew this didn't work all the time, but thought it prevented squabbles. He felt it was more do as you wish now.

"It's called that so if you always do it, life is more likely to stay golden. If not, it tarnishes," Mark said. "Pure gold doesn't tarnish, so means more to wearers."

"Many problems are from ignoring how we affect others," said Jan.

"By avoiding others who antagonize, I feel at ease," Will said. He watched movies and read to help him make good decisions.

"It's all staying close to the positive so negative won't harm you," Cy said.

CHAPTER 38

"So we avoided getting near those money and coin sacks at Doc's house. Until we know what's going on there, that's the only way to play it safe," said Mark.

"Few at school would ignore the money. Some would touch it to see if it were real," said Will. "Because it's not mine, I wouldn't have."

"For years in Tokyo, Japan, word was that anyone could leave a business door unlocked and leave it. When they returned, nothing was missing," Cy said.

"The Japanese believe one has to work hard to have. It's stealing another's labor, not the item, when something's taken without paying for it," said Mark.

In many other countries, lying, cheating and stealing are more serious offenses than here. It can result in higher fines or jail time that can't be worked away by community service. Living in the U.S. is truly freer than elsewhere.

"In music, you shouldn't have to pay to make your songs

succeed. A record label covers all the costs in making you available to the public," Cy said. "That's like paying for your own labor, and no one is likely to do that. But initially, you may have to pay for recording your songs to prove your ability to music producers."

"If you are good enough to have a singing career, the companies come to you or through an agent who looks for talent, such as who will visit Greentown during the 'Annie' performance. You may have to send a demo recording to an agent if they hear of you in some other way, like a newspaper article or magazine story. But you don't shop to have your talent heard," Will said.

In developing talent, youth has an advantage. Sometimes older people make it in a few areas of art, writing, poetry, and playing a musical instrument; but for athletics, singing, acting, ballet or dancing, to make it as a professional, one must begin young.

"Didn't you tell us, Gramps, that people called sharks could take advantage of young people who don't know how the music business works?" Jan asked.

"In the old days it was more common. 'Agents' seeing little talent in a person asked for money in advance to record and promote them. They may have promised great things like a recording contract with a big company to lure you. But, they had no contacts to offer you. Now, most people with talent know how music works and have family, lawyers and common sense to assure it never happens. Unlike most other jobs, they get paid very well for being great at what they do," Cy said.

"Shows like 'American Idol' have helped people like me know the ropes and made young people who have talent work extremely hard at being their best. So their chances of making it sooner or later are far better," said Will. "It also gives hope to those who weren't sure how to have hope. There's light in the night now."

"When I was young, many who heard Dad sing at church told him he could be like Elvis. But for reaching that goal, he wasn't sure of where or who to go to. So he and Mom had that dream for years and didn't know how to bring it about. Recording agents even came, but Dad stayed in his company to get his retirement. We could have been known to the world otherwise," Jan said.

"If you have friends and family, as Will does, who know you can do it and they work as hard as he does to help him make it, there's more chance at it," said Cy.

"Every one person working with you multiplies your chance to get there several times over having even one against you," Jan said.

"Loving what you do is critical; having others around you love it is the rocket to the stars," said Mark. "After all, Dad and I are not just a carpenter and an architect but the men who can do just about anything with a project." Their work was special because they had spent so many years at it.

"From all over the world you get calls but don't like flying most of the time, so you've stayed local except a few national jobs for charity in the past, right Gramps?" Jan asked.

"Sure. Some years ago we did jobs in Africa, Asia and Japan. Then word got out, and the four corners of the earth were writing and calling. That was right before Mark met you, of course," Cy said. A grin creased his somber face.

"The more friends and family one has, the better. None of us do it alone. For a book to succeed, a publisher must accept it. Singers and musicians perform in concert halls and recording studios. They seldom own those places, but are there due to their talents. If they're athletes, a team has to pay them, except for individual sports like golf or tennis, where large sponsors help pay the winners. The players work their way up until they are allowed to compete once they play well enough to be in a tournament. Actors have to read for parts and show how they perform," Will said.

The most difficult task anyone has is to find work to make it worth doing. If fortune smiles upon you with the blessing of choosing work that you love and giving you the talent to learn it or it's partially a natural talent, life can be more of a pleasure than a burden.

"You can't rest on what you've done in the past," Jan said. She thought how her girls in the program worked so hard to improve.

"Yes, even the most accomplished talents maintain high levels until they leave due to age or illness. Bob Hope and George Burns were good examples. Both just kept it up until they couldn't perform or travel anymore," Cy said.

"They gave more to the country than most people in history and were over ninety when they couldn't perform anymore," said Jan.

"The positive attitude kept them going so long. They always knew that they'd go on. Bob Hope's health gave out, and he fought it, so it didn't best him until he was really up in age. George Burns continued until he couldn't. With Hope, the public, especially the troops, loved him so much that he drew great strength from them. George Burns thrived on being in the public," said Mark.

"It was like a mirror for Bob. The love he showed to others reflected back to him. In many people's lives reaching out often makes life better." Jan said.

These comedians are ones who are mostly unknown to anyone under age forty but lived longer than most comedians now will. Burns was 100 and Hope was almost 100.

They not only lived long because they gave much to others, but they loved what they did and were paid well for it. To them, every day was sunshine, and they drew life from that light. Only a few people in the world can gain all they had. But we can try. It takes faith, finding something we love to do daily and working hard to stay useful to others.

CHAPTER 39

"Life is all about doing our best to extend love out as often as possible. Each of us who does it multiplies the effect in the world. In this day, it may be harder to show joy, since there's a lot of stress, but when we do, it makes us feel better in ourselves," Cy said.

"It's really like we are what we do. Avoiding anything negative means it can't damage your ability to show love to others," Mark said.

"Smiling is a lot easier than frowning," Will said. "Your face has to work harder to frown than to smile."

"That's close, son," said Jan. "What I think you meant is that the muscles have to work much harder to frown than to smile."

"But the idea is that you feel a lot better inside to smile. It's contagious," Cy said.

Common smiles are uncommon now, but when they are there, it makes loads easier to bear. Finding at least one joyful event a day is an accomplishment. The McGinns, being Scottish, had to learn to smile. But it meant change and took years.

"When you smile, people stay around you and are drawn to you a lot more," said Mark. Many days he couldn't smile thinking about work, the world and others' problems.

"Because we spend so much time together, all the sweet stuff stays around, and the sour thoughts go someplace else," said Will. "Guess that's why I don't want sugar too often. A coating of happy love keeps me full."

"Gramps, didn't you say that what makes church so special is that there are far more people who pass around the sweets instead of holding them?" asked Mark. Some churches did little of that, Mark noticed. So he never returned. Feeling alone and unwanted, he met Jan when he was invited to Cy's church. So it was like another home when he went.

"Yeah, we shake hands, smile and hug as much as we can. Out in the world some don't get that in a month. When all of you go with me, you treasure that." It didn't happen that often, as they were mostly busy.

"We're going to be there more often from now on. Mark and I have talked about it, and Will said he wants to be there with you, Gramps," offered Jan.

"It gives me that tingle in my head and warmth in my heart," said Will. "And for at least a few days after I go it keeps me smiling. Then I want to recharge and start all over."

"Others glow in the face when I tell them how it makes me feel," said Mark. "Then I ask them to visit soon, and some say they'll try."

"Going to church can make you live longer," Jan said.

"It's the social strength that you gather amongst people of like mind," said Mark.

"If there's any proof of it, that's me," said Cy. "And in there every week are more older people. Younger ones are really losing out on it."

Many churches are mostly older people because church is not a 'cool' idea to those younger. Young people bring young ones, and it takes young ideas to make church a place to be. You have to want to go since most people aren't forced to as schools do.

Sometimes young people or adults may find the only hope is in church. Losses of any kind have brought on a need to go when there had never been before. Going before a problem or need occurs has been the best way to assure the needs are met when one attends.

"How many kids often go, Gramps?" asked Will.

"Oh, quite a few, but it's most often because mom and dad push them," Cy said.

For years the McGinns attended church, although Cy went the most. The rest of the family worshipped together at home. Their souls would soothe their hunger.

"It's ridiculous that a child is squeezed to go to church," said Jan.

"God makes his own way into our lives but along different paths," said Cy.

"We only follow them," Jan added.

"Many kids I know could use church," Will said. "Talking them into it can seem impossible."

"To draw them must be something such as music they like along with a good youth minister," said Cy.

"For many, music is a major drawing card," said Mark. "That's new Christian music."

"A young youth minister is needed," said Cy.

"Yeah, we need someone who sees our world," said Will. "Fewer religious books are even written for us."

"Once you're headed in a positive direction, you'll keep on track as long as you avoid negatives," said Cy.

CHAPTER 40

"An article in the Greentown Press was titled, 'Young People, Their Influences and Positive Directions,'" Cy said. This supported everything the McGinns believed and gave them hope for the future.

"We need emotional, physical and spiritual support," said Mark.

"There's no day that goes by where I don't use faith," Will said. "There's no way that I could believe only in myself to get by." Faith means different things to different people. Sometimes it's positive thoughts, sometimes prayers, other times feeling family or friends will help with problems.

"Many successful people admit that faith made them what they are," Jan said.

"That's what separates us as human beings from all other creatures," said Cy. "We rely on faith to give us strength."

"Not having faith would make me feel alone in the world." Mark said.

"Much of the world seems to rely on themselves for survival. But looking outside for power is beneficial," said Jan.

"Many of my teachers say they have faith, pray and go to church every week and admit that it would be impossible to start the week without it." Will could feel the strength that his teachers gave him. He'd never be lost or alone with a light shining to lead him along the path.

"If you look at the stars, moon, oceans, mountains, that is faith in action," Jan said. "Those are all things that we had no part in creating but exist to keep us happy." Her eyes glowed and sparks shot from them into the air.

"To some people, faith in a pet, their jobs or other people take the place of spiritual faith," Cy said. "It shouldn't be that way, but whatever gives a feeling of ease at the time is where faith concentrates."

The quickest way for many to lose faith is for things in life to go suddenly wrong. A bad test grade when you studied hard, losing a friend or parent who passes, losing your first job or any job, an accident that hurt you, lacking enough money to take care of yourself, rejection by someone are examples. It is then that others with faith may help you gain it back. You may struggle to do it alone. Look for others at those times.

"In my singing I have faith. It's what I'm using to get ahead in life," said Will.

"That's a strong belief in your abilities, not faith," Mark said. "Faith is a belief in the unseen, and you can see your skills as a singer."

Creative skills come from outside faith, being in tune with what the world wants, Will knew. But the creation itself is done by us, from our daily living. It is who we meet, where we go, what we do. Many give credit to themselves, but that's not honest.

"A good artist takes from the scenes around him. An

author will sense people and situations much better than average. Actors must become the character portrayed. Singers must open up the hearts of those who listen to them," said Jan.

"Mustard seed faith. So small, but it can move mountains," added Will. "Jesus had it, Job did, and Peter had it to walk on water."

"Believing anything can be done is faith," Mark said.

"Seeing others succeed can either increase or decrease faith depending on what has happened to us," Cy remarked.

"If we succeed, seeing others do well often supports us. But if we have a hard time, it may create anxiety and hinder us," Mark added.

"When I saw Clay Aiken make it, my effort increased," said Will.

"Do people with a lot of money have more faith than those with less?" Jan inquired. "It's easier to feel it will go well with less worry about expenses."

"Sometimes yes, maybe no," Mark said.

"The foundation of all faith is family, where belief in self, others and God begins," knew Cy.

"The ministry gives strength to the family so faith in God more easily occurs," said Jan.

"You have to take the music to the world to make it succeed," said Will.

"Faith is like that. It is far better that others have it, too," said Cy.

"Although Jesus had ultimate faith, He still surrounded himself with the disciples," said Jan.

"It shows faith when you continue to pray. Whether it is or isn't answered, a belief that it'll be answered for the better is where strong faith comes in," said Will.

"Going on and never giving up. That's what faith is to me," said Mark.

CHAPTER 41

"For some people, they may lose the will to carry on when prayers seem unanswered. Working as hard to pray as to study the Word, we expect the same benefit," said Jan.

"Hearing people say how prayer has helped in some ways even after working at it is strength. Maybe it wasn't answered right away. But it may happen," said Cy.

"It's senseless when bad things happen even with constant prayer for something or someone who is more faithful than average," Will said.

"If we could throw away and only keep good stuff, many would rejoice." Mark said.

"Some problems make us think how to solve things. Too many can damage," said Jan.

"Pastor Jaba says that some problems force people to rely on each other, like floods or earthquakes. Others make us look at ourselves and pray for strength and wisdom to deal with it," Cy said.

They all looked at their lives and how they handled situations. Jan was guiding young girls. Will knew he had constant practice to make the songs work. Cy and Mark always built around obstacles.

"When I sing, I do the best that I can and know that it's all that can be expected. If I bring joy to the audience so that they smile, the right attitude is there," Will said.

"With top quality we build and will forever," Cy and Mark admitted.

"When girls need help, I move them ahead, never stagnate," said Jan.

"Everyone has their own way to reach goals and maintain faith while doing so. For some, they rely on prayer before they take any action. Others make their own decisions or discuss it with friends and family, but success can only come with hard work, perseverance and focusing on the goal," Mark said.

"I see now that we can't rely on income from the sack of cash to provide our primary happiness," Cy said.

"If we gain it by default, some of life will be easier but not all of it," said Mark.

"There's no way that I'd want to have it given to me. Unless I could be sure that I'd only be able to spend a little at a time," Will said.

Some of the people have been spoiled or given too much by parents when the work has not really been done to earn it. That's one of the greatest hazards to success in the world. It's the consistent giving only with a price attached that breeds success. When you look at anyone who has reached most milestones in life, few have been spoiled.

"We want our goal in life to be assisting others. Then any happiness we gain will come naturally," said Cy.

"To assist others, we need to be grateful for what we

have. Then we can get out of ourselves for others," said Mark.

Jan said, "I'm glad my work's doing for those who can't pay for what they get."

"All the thanks one needs to have is seeing others do well because of what you did for them," said Will.

"If every person who worked did one hour of volunteer work a week, the world would change," said Cy. "Working for free teaches that it's not pay that makes you valuable but what you do to serve others."

"Few who give a hand to others at no cost dislike it. But, when they work at their regular job and think they're paid too little, they can go off in anger," Jan said.

"It's said there are many volunteers in the U.S., but I'm not sure if you see it obviously," said Mark. "It's not glorified to make the volunteers proud like a pro athlete."

"If the whole world moved in that direction, there may be fewer wars, crime, poverty, emotional pain, divorce or other harsh realities," said Cy.

CHAPTER 42

"Catch the phone, hon," said Mark, as it rang that evening.

Jan answered the phone, and it was Doctor McKenzie finally able to let her know about the money that Cy and Mark had seen left at his property. He was terse and explained that no one whom he had spoken with, all authorities, claimed to know the owner. It wasn't stolen, and the van that dropped it had vanished. So he told her some surprising news. "Jan, we can't find an owner for that cash, and I've been given approval to dispose of it in any manner that I choose. Since your family was the first to see it, it should go to them," he said.

"Doctor, Cy or Mark will have to deal with this," Jan said. "For me this is way too much of a change to our way of life. Mark, you need to talk to the doctor about this," Jan whispered, as she handed him the phone.

"Hi, Doc. We'll call Pastor Jaba to see what he feels is best." Doc explained that he should call immediately, since it was early. "Yes, it's only seven o'clock, so we can reach him at home. This is a real test for our values, and we had discussed what to do with the unearned wealth. Thanks for calling, and we'll get back with you," said Mark. Then he hung up and called the pastor.

"Hello Pastor Jaba," said Mark. "So to speak, that money we discovered has come to haunt us. Doc McKenzie has offered it to us, but we need moral guidance here. You feel that a trust where the church will allot certain amounts per month will be best. It sounds wise, and then you and the deacons can use income as you need to." Jaba agreed and Mark continued, "Great, I'll call Doc McKenzie back on this." Then he hung up.

He called Doc and told him of his decision. "We're giving to our minister for his program. Their bank and members are in charge of what to do with the funds. How much is it, by the way?" Doc told him and he gasped for breath. "Ten million dollars! That requires people who are used to dealing with large funds. I'm glad we're making this decision. Pastor Jaba decided that he wanted to be sure that Cy was well compensated for his honesty and there would be time to enjoy what we have found," Mark said. "We'll call you later if we need to," he said, hanging up.

Calling Pastor Jaba back with the amount of gold, Cy was told, "Cy, we know that you don't want any bulk amount of the cash value. But up front we've decided to give you at least one million. Then out of eight more million, we'll give you two hundred thousand a year so that you would have about forty or more years of compensation. The church will keep one million in the trust for us," Jaba said.

"Pastor, we prefer a hundred thousand annually with an option for up to the higher amount. We don't want it to influence us negatively and feel this is better," Cy said.

"I understand, since you've been living on less so long, it could be too much of a change for you too fast," Jaba said.

He felt that most of the family could absorb the change but was concerned about Will. Even Bill Gates was going to limit the amount of direct income to his son so that he could learn responsibility. For them this could allow a better standard of living but was too fast of a change.

"I think Coon may want a little different dog house, but even he shouldn't be spoiled," said Cy. "I might get him a few extra toys or treats and a better leash but no luxuries any more than the rest of us."

For their personal account, Sheila, the pastor's wife, suggested that they would have a personal limit of twenty-five thousand a year. In the past Pastor Jaba overspent, and Sheila had to put a clamp on it. For the church he'd buy toys for the toddler room, like Romper Rats that were bouncing balls you sat on and hopped around. They had faces of rats, slithery tails and scared parents. He got Slinkys for members, hoping that tossing them hand to hand during services would keep them awake. For the bus ministry, he got aooga horns on buses that had whole neighborhoods up in arms.

Sheila felt like she was raising a child. Jaba was into games to keep his people amused. Board games, cards, computer games and ones he made up. It all became a big joke, and he couldn't stop them. "We're doing the right thing here for all of us," Sheila said as she got on the phone, "so that no blame is put on anyone with our attitude." Then she gave the phone back to the pastor.

"Sheila arranges our finances and keeps my wallet closed. When we shop I give it to her, and she often returns it a few days later!" Jaba said.

"Well, Jan does it with Mark, too. He takes no time

to shop. Going to the city, he gets wild and sees what he neither needs nor wants," Cy said. "Before Will was born he returned with a trunk of baby's goods and women's wear. None of the clothing was maternity wear. He felt so foolish."

"To let Jan buy everything is wise. She wouldn't goof like that," said Pastor Jaba.

"Jan has little urge to shop, except for girls in her organization. But she'll go out of her way for them," Cy said.

"With her blessings she's cautious," said Pastor Jaba.

"That's true. Mark and I will hold our blessings, except we'll provide for others to start businesses. Will gets studio time and voice lessons," Cy said. "Hold on, we'll be over in a few minutes and discuss this more in person."

"Okay, see you shortly," Jaba said, as he hung up the phone.

CHAPTER 43

Cy and Mark had left immediately, drove up to Jaba's driveway, knocked, and were ushered into the open living room. Jaba began the conversation.

"We'll do more outreach in town," said Pastor Jaba. "Some years ago, we went door to door and asked parents and their children to come to church."

"Without buses to bring the little ones, parents failed to respond," Sheila said.

"Then we dropped Bibles at those same houses with our programs in them and personal letters asking them to attend. Our children made drawings for the children in the families," said Pastor Jaba.

"And they didn't come when you followed with calls," Cy said.

"No, because they wanted the kids to go first and test the church for them," said Jaba.

"Any buses available for them?" Cy asked.

"We couldn't afford them," said Jaba.

"Now you can buy a few buses and try again," Cy said.

"We'll only get a forty passenger first, then more if needed," said Jaba.

"Don't worry about a new one. Mark and I can fancy up inside and outside," Cy said.

"Another church has one with scriptures all over it for attention and their telephone number on it," said Jaba.

Buses are not just for public transportation for cities and for ferrying kids to schools. They've proved to be the most valuable asset to a church, especially in poor areas where parents may not have cars. They could be called Motors for the Master. It can be the best way for adults and children to get to know one another and make friends.

"We have some audio equipment, and I've got some CD's of low-volume chimes. With the audio will be a hood speaker. A switch for the bus door, when it opens as we stop at each house, sets the chimes off," Cy said.

"Make copies of the chime CD with our phone number for the kids' parents and give another Bible," said Jaba.

"Let's have a Conestoga wagon and horse with a small barn at the church," Cy said.

"Wagon rides around the grounds may keep their interest in coming back," Sheila said.

"With some smaller farm animals for a petting zoo, we may encourage stewardship and family activity together," Cy added.

"Then at Christmas, a genuine manger scene instead of a plastic or ceramic one. Feeding animals of the manger scene is for the kids," Jaba suggested.

"Adults volunteers can dress as Joseph and Mary and give flyers to visitors to draw them in. On Sundays children can assist," Sheila said.

CHAPTER 44

"The money's not ours yet, so why all these ideas about what we're going to do with it?" Cy asked. "There's no reason to have hopes too high only to have them dashed."

"Well, with a written letter bearing the mayor of Greentown's signature, the state seal and the governor's signature, in ninety days the money could be banked. To begin it's only a million," Jaba said.

"Speaking about that. What about that wealthy auto dealership owner who attends once every few weeks? He gives a hundred thousand a year, but that's very little for him," Mark said.

"We'd rather him give more time to us, since he seems to value that more," Jaba said.

"He can drive the bus with all the kids bouncing in time to his fortunate hair flapping in the wind," said Cy.

"Some large bills may float out the windows, since he

stuffs his top jacket pockets, his shoes, his shirt, and he tapes them to his wrists," Jaba said.

"Surprised he hasn't been robbed if he went outside of Greentown as a jackal," Mark cracked.

"Oh, the ones on his wrists he finally stuffs in his side pocket. With a fancy alarm system and wires through his clothing, when they're touched, it sets a squealer off that says, 'call the law, call the law, he just robbed my house,'" said Jaba.

"Too bad he feels lost without carrying all that money. We don't want a lot at the time to warp reality. Howard Hughes pushed his mind to the limit, but he became so wealthy that he lost part of himself and never found it." Cy sighed.

Will and Jan drove up and strolled to knock on the door. Jaba's voice greeted them when they pressed the intercom button.

"Yes, come on in, Jan and Will. We'll discuss a few things about my funds," he said.

CHAPTER 45

Opening the door when they heard the lock-open buzz, they walked into the office. As they sat, the pastor locked his hands together behind his neck, leaning back in his chair. He grinned at them and then cracked a straight face.

"How are you, and hope life is treating you well," Jaba said. "We're still dealing with this money but shall figure it out." Leaning forward, he waved his arms in front of him like a magician.

"With some of the money I'd like to build a recording studio for poor, talented kids," Will said. "And I'd practice there."

"What does Mark want to do with the money?" Jaba asked.

"Same as Cy wants, a business helping other people start businesses. Guess it runs in the family," Jan said.

"That's okay. It's important that the gift is used to benefit other people, not how it is used," Jaba said.

"For anyone who listens, I'll sing. Even if I don't succeed at recording right away, it's for others," Will said.

"Do anything first for your own joy to give others a talent," Cy said. "Success is doing your best, regardless of outcome. Because the heart goes into it, someone's best is always quality."

"I only have the best me to give the church," Jaba said. "If not, people wouldn't follow."

"All of us have to reach for new goals. As soon as one is achieved, run for the next one. Then we succeed by living a long and happy life," Cy said.

"Looking outward and never inward is the rule to achieve. We can never be the master of ourselves. Only God can do that," said Jaba.

Jan, Will, Mark and Cy knew how they felt. Being part of the McGinn family was their greatest love, after God. It mattered not if they had to work or had wealth. The money would make life easier but couldn't guarantee happiness. A family couldn't either. But it was as close as you could come to a life of joy.